LOST
AMERICAN
FICTION

*Edited by* Matthew J. Bruccoli

The title for this series, "Lost American Fiction," is unsatisfactory. A more accurate series title would be "Forgotten American Works of Fiction That Deserve a New Public"—which states the rationale for reprinting these titles. No claim is made that we are resuscitating lost masterpieces, although the first work in the series, Edith Summers Kelley's *Weeds,* may qualify. We are simply reprinting some works that are worth rereading because they are now social documents (*Dry Martini*) or literary documents (*The Professors Like Vodka*). It isn't that simple, for Southern Illinois University Press is a scholarly publisher; and we do have serious ambitions for the series. We expect that these titles will revive some books and authors from undeserved obscurity, and that the series will therefore plug some of the holes in American literary history. Of course, we hope to find an occasional lost masterpiece.

M. J. B.

*Harold Loeb*

# THE
# PROFESSORS
# LIKE VODKA

*

With an Afterword
by the Author

Southern Illinois University Press
Carbondale and Edwardsville
Feffer & Simons, Inc.
London and Amsterdam

Library of Congress Cataloging in Publication Data
Loeb, Harold, 1891-
    The professors like vodka.
    (Lost American fiction)
    Reprint, with a new afterword, of the ed. published by Boni
& Liveright, New York.
    I.  Title.
PZ3.L8238Pr10        [PS3523.0278]        813'.5'2        73-16121
ISBN 0-8093-0664-6

To

My Friend

MALCOLM COWLEY

*THE PROFESSORS LIKE VODKA*

# THE PROFESSORS
# LIKE VODKA

## CHAPTER ONE

PROFESSOR MERCADO was not the
kind of man whom strangers and casual
acquaintances usually addressed. His wide,
firm mouth and solid chin were forbidding in
repose. Nor was his friend, Professor Halsey, though of a mild appearance, easy to approach. Yet the young man, who had been
eyeing them insistently from a nearby table,
suddenly rose and slouched into a chair along-
side.

"Remember me?" he said. "I'm Hamilton
Corey. Used to take one of your courses—
English 14a. Let me see. It was entitled
'American Literature from the Beginnings till
1850.' You gave me C+. Your name's Pro-

[ 9 ]

fessor Mercado. I'm fried. Don't mind, do you, if I order another drink?"

Undoubtedly, Mercado thought, Paris has a demoralizing effect on young Americans. But his former pupil was still speaking.

"There goes Sam Hewitt. Tough luck for poor old Sam. They 'rested him, gave him two weeks to leave Paris. I'm just like that.

"That is, I'm not being put out, but I have to leave. Time's up. Four years in Paris, Beaux-Arts and all that. Graduated. Going home. Got a job in an architect's office. Be respectable. Must see Vera. Countess Adranova. Can't, not till midnight. Relatives come first.

"Good-by, youth. Understand, I'm not complaining. I'm twenty-seven now, time to settle down 'n' find a nice girl. Maybe I'll even like her. Going to be a success, big success, design country houses to look just like Petit Trianon. *Adieu, au revoir*, so long Paris, *je t'embrasse la main*. Anyhow I've lived.

"You're a Jew, aren't you, Mercado? And what about you? I forget your name, never took your courses . . . Halsey, did you say? Well, you sound like a New Englander. I

lived. You never lived. Imagine either of
you getting pie-eyed and rolling in the gutter.
Imagine you having an affair with Vera! Can't.
No life in you, nothing but Greensborough
University. In ten years I'll be as dead as you,
but anyhow I'll have something to remember.

"Why don't you try just once? Caveau
Ukranien. Ask for Vera. I'll meet you at
twelve, no, twelve-thirty. On second thought
you'd better keep away from Vera. Here's five
francs to pay for my drinks. So long."

He rose and stumbled toward a taxi. "As
if we knew nothing," Halsey grunted. "It
makes me a little, well, angry to think of these
boys. I've been fried, too, if I am a New England Puritan. Well, what do you say, John,
shall we go home?"

"I suppose we might as well," Professor
Mercado reluctantly answered. "A Russian
Countess! Do you know I think, sometimes,
that we're not getting all we should out of
this city."

"Well, I'm game," said Halsey, "there's a
taxicab now. The five francs just about cover
the drinks—

"Taxi!" He stopped the cab and asked in

careful Greensborough French: *"Vous connaissez le . . . le Caveau Ukranien?"*

"Wait a minute," said Mercado, "don't go off like that. Let's talk it over."

"All right." Halsey waved the driver to go on. "Shall we have another drink?" And then Mercado changed the subject and never even mentioned the Caveau until three days later.

They had decided, after a long talk, to leave town and seek, by way of two bicycles, the exotic atmosphere which was so provokingly elusive, and had dropped into silence.

Suddenly Mercado sat up straight, as if he had just made an important decision, and said: "Let us, before we go, pay one visit to Montmartre."

"But that will be worse," Halsey objected, "we don't have to go to Paris to see our nouveau riche countrymen cavort."

"I know," Mercado answered, "but I've a reason."

"Which is?"

At first he would not give his reason, because, as he said, it was so trivial. Finally, after a bit of coaxing, he explained that he wanted to look over Hamilton Corey's Russian Countess.

Halsey wanted to know why, if he was so curious, he hadn't suggested that they look into this affair sooner. For unless he'd mixed his dates, Hamilton was scheduled to sail the next day.

"I've been thinking about it," Mercado replied, "ever since he told us about her." They had come to Europe and were fussing about with a lot of people just like those they had left at home. Here was a chance to expand their experience. Why should they pass it up? "Of course," he added, "I quite expect another disillusionment."

"Don't fool yourself," Halsey replied, "you don't want to visit the Caveau to broaden your education. It's Hamilton's warning that's got under your skin. If he'd wanted to introduce you to Vera, you'd have turned him down."

"Perhaps," Mercado answered. And then, after a pause, as if the question had been settled, "Let's pay for our drinks and go."

After all, Halsey thought, as they selected an open taxi, it's pleasant crossing the city on a

summer night. He was not averse to riding
through the warm air. At night the yellow
lights by the Seine with their long comet tails,
and the ghostly nimbi which crowned the monu-
ments, won even Mercado's admiration. Not
even he could ride over the glistening surface
of the Place de la Concorde without feeling
the nobility of the formal arrangement.

John Mercado had taken a dislike to Parisian
architecture. He inveighed against the studied
regularity of the city plan; it reminded him of
a schoolboy design. Except in the old quarters,
where the quaintness of bygone ages invested
the stained walls and wry windows, no scope
was left for the imagination. The several
styles were doubtless good, though he thought
even that was open to question, but when sla-
vishly followed the element of surprise was
lost. He liked to find, in town as well as country, features which startled one by their loveliness or grotesqueness. Now New York, for
instance . . . And he would go into a pane-
gyric over skyscrapers, Colonial ironwork, sun-
sets beneath the elevated.

In the beginning Halsey had argued with
him, pointing out various Gothic gables and

Renaissance porticos which even the guide-books had failed to note, but his points were lightly dismissed and he surrendered, after a while, from inertia. He felt that if Mercado, when in Paris, could see only the sublimity of the Bush Building, it was Mercado's loss, not his. Besides, in a sense, John wasn't sincere. He just couldn't resist a paradoxical argument.

The vacation was not proving a success. Probably they had hoped for too much. On inheriting a legacy which was too small to warrant reinvesting, Mercado had convinced his friend that a visit to Europe was just what they needed. It had not been difficult. Halsey was more than half persuaded before an argument had been produced. And Mercado had been eloquent. "Our minds," he said, "are being stultified by monotony. Fifteen years on a university campus would turn a dragon-fly into an oyster. We must not refuse this chance to freshen our outlooks by the stimulus of contrast." As Halsey had saved up a little money and was bored by the thought of another summer at Lake George, the prospect filled him with enthusiasm. They spent the balance of the spring term dusting their memories and re-vising their plans. Both had crossed the ocean the year they graduated, and never afterwards.

Their holiday was disappointing. The sights and gayeties, remembered from before the war, seemed to have become a little tawdry. Mercado felt that the capacity for enjoyment is probably as considerable in the staid college professor, with his years of routine behind him, as in the undergraduate, but that his demands are more exacting. He is not so easily satisfied by the superficially glamorous. He looks behind the scenes, analyzing and reflecting upon the pastimes, which, in youth, he spontaneously accepted. Not that either Halsey or himself was prudish, quite the contrary, but they had become settled in their ways and critical of divagations.

They were bored. The permanent American colony of Montparnasse was not so different from the little theater group at home. Individual eccentricities had been allowed to develop, as American public opinion would never have permitted, and morals were more openly lax, but if the exiles got any good from their freedom, Mercado was unable to discover it. He remarked, after spending an evening behind little growing piles of beer saucers, that the only effect the famous city seemed to have on his countrymen was to break down their conventional reserve. Never had he listened to such indiscriminate, self-indulgent, revelatory fragments of autobiography. "They get more kick telling their troubles," he concluded, "than they do out of suffering them." Of course there were exceptions. Hard-working, ambitious writers, serious painters, as well as charming student loafers who really relished the chain of revelry. However, his main impression was that the Americans of the quarter fell roughly into two classes: failures, who found the tolerance of the older civilization more comfortable than the sharp edges of their own land, and sentimentalists, who enjoyed spouting the platitudes they had gleaned from third-rate sex and travel literature.

Halsey was struck, on looking back, by the curious relevancy of this criticism. For Mercado eventually proved his point by undergoing in Paris the same relaxation which he had observed in the residents. They had known each other nearly sixteen years, having become intimate during a post-graduate course on the beginnings of American literature. They possessed a mutual enthusiasm for research work though their approach was as different as their temperaments. In those days Mercado had been very reserved, holding himself aloof from the gregarious frolics of his fellows. As a result he had not been popular. However, his high forehead and penetrating eyes suggested the sensitiveness of his personality. It was several months before Halsey broke through his diffidence, the cause of his apparent austerity, and got to know the likable individual it concealed. Even then, Halsey discovered, only when they were alone did he unbend his austere manner and become human.

They had been appointed, on completing their studies, to the same college. As the years passed Mercado had gained more self-assurance and had learned how to mix freely with his associates. He had been well liked by most of the Faculty, for no one was more stimulating in an intimate talk. In time Halsey quite forgot his initial impression and would not have described him as more reserved or shy than the average man.

Just the same when Paris, or more accurately,

when Cléopâtre had worked up his emotions with the result that he revealed without reservation the intricate and personal volutions of his sensitive mind, Halsey recalled with surprise his original estimate of his friend's character and decided in future to distrust first impressions.

Halsey was lying back in his corner, musing over the old civilization which had perpetuated its grandiose dreams in stone, when he was disturbed by a remark which showed that Mercado's mind was far from the subject of his own meditations.

"I've always wanted to really know a Russian," he exclaimed. "They are the only Europeans capable of genuine passion. All the rest are emasculated by the cynicism which overtakes every civilization of a certain age."

"You'll probably find them much like everybody else," Halsey lazily rejoined, irritated by having his pleasant reverie interrupted.

"Don't you believe it." The voice was unnecessarily emphatic. What, Halsey wondered, has worked up his feelings? Surely there is nothing unusual about a couple of Americans visiting a Russian cabaret. That's what they're run for.

"I should," Mercado continued, "hate the very name Russian. The impression their atrocities against my race made on me as a child is still as vivid . . ." And he went on to explain that his mind did not work that way. He was sure that if they had all the facts they would realize the pogroms had been inevitable. No one had proved more conclusively than Dostoievsky that to understand is to forgive. And besides he did not see any reason why he should be concerned with an economic situation in which he had had no part.

Halsey kept silent. John Mercado, in all the years they had known each other, had been so lacking in racial consciousness that Halsey usually forgot he was of different stock than himself. Of course they had occasionally speculated on racial differences and on the subject of prejudice, but idly, impersonally, as if the question was of no more moment than relativity, or any other abstract preoccupation.

His heat astonished Halsey. It made him feel that Mercado's racial roots were deeper than he had suspected.

"I know what's the matter with you," Mercado continued, looking at Halsey with his searching eyes, "you're afraid, afraid of being out of place. . . ." And he attacked mercilessly their timorous acceptance of the professorial state of mind. He, for one, did not feel called upon to become a mummy just because his vocation, for nine months of the year, was to inculcate overgrown schoolboys with embalmed classics. He didn't feel dead yet and wasn't going to pretend to be dead. Halsey was astonished at his friend's incoherence. It was unusual, in fact unique. "Why didn't you speak to that little blonde girl on the boat whose laugh you liked?" Mercado asked. "Because you were afraid of appearing undignified. Bosh! I'm sick of being a staid professor. We're not going to live forever." He was no better, he confessed, than Halsey. He had wanted to join the young people's frolics and he hadn't done so. Why? Because he was too diffident. Because he feared being ridiculous. The fool he had been. A charming woman had looked at him during the entire crossing and he had never dared speak to her until they were jostled together getting off the boat train. And he hadn't taken her address even then, though she would have been only too happy to have given it to him. Now they were complaining because their vacation was disillusioning. "It's our fault," he insisted, "we think of ourselves as ambulant fogies and, as a result, are accepted as such. But we're not. We're delightful young sports, out for a good time and sure of finding it. Do you see what I mean, Halsey? It's our frame of mind that's all wrong. Not our age or our personalities. And we can change it if we want to bad enough . . ."

Halsey was thinking, as his friend spoke, that what Mercado said was probably true enough for him, good-looking, vital, magnetic, but as for himself . . .

However, before he had a chance to reply, they drew up to an imposing structure in the very heart of Montmartre on which a row of electric bulbs spelled "Caveau Ukranien."

An impressive uniform ushered them through the door. In the barbaric vestibule a Cossack smoked an insolent cigarette against the hat and coat counter. Music percolated through various openings. They mounted the stairs. A long room, where red chairs and tables were lined against the walls like tomatoes against a festooned trellis, took them in. The light, bustle and animation confused them for the moment. A buxom woman, confident and self-possessed, asked if they wanted a table.

"Where's the bar?" Mercado demanded, not wanting to start with champagne.

"This way."

She smiled amiably. A square alcove opened off the long room at the end of which a small bar was tended by a young man in white, who seemed, in his chaste costume, incongruously dressed. They took possession of the only vacant stools and, from the comparative stability of their perches, began to recover their self-possession.

The barkeeper exhibited prehensile teeth as he took their order. They began to distinguish individuals. The orchestra was jazzing a Russian folk melody.

Several drinks were swallowed. A belted nonchalant Cossack executed a sword dance. The buxom lady, who turned out to be the French hostess of the upper floor, chatted with them pleasantly and accepted their offer of a drink by ordering an orangeade. They listened meditatively to the *Volga Boat Song*, that most mournful dirge. It seemed to animate the crude but forceful frescoes which overlaid the walls. The prevailing color scheme, inherited from Byzantine icons, assumed a savage splendor.

A phantasmic mood had taken possession of the professors which made the past seem unreal. The sensation was pleasant. The sloughing off of their reserve released an emotion, as unexpected as it was delightful. Halsey would never have believed that he was susceptible to this kind of influence. Teachers, perhaps, know less about themselves than other people. If any one had foretold that such primitive revelry would hold him, he would have laughed. He supposed that the orgiastic impulses are never completely atrophied. At least the craze for jazz seemed to prove this.

A diminutive English girl slid in between their stools like a cockney expletive. She had two song and dance numbers which she gave every evening on each of the three floors. Mercado asked her to dance. Halsey followed suit. She surely could dance. She became beautiful in their eyes and they made pretty schoolboy speeches, delighted at the chance to turn an English phrase. She did not take their compliments too seriously.

"Look!" Mercado exclaimed, seizing his friend's arm. An informal procession was passing between the alcove and the dancing floor. The Russian entertainers were coming upstairs for a recess. They carried themselves, in their exotic costumes, with dignity, as if they were feudal hosts passing among their motley retainers. Tall women in old court costumes with white fan-like headdresses. Cossacks, wasp-waisted and shod in soft leather boots. Dancers in gaudy gypsy dresses. Slowly they went by, one after the other. Halsey was particularly struck by a beautiful woman with irregular bewitching features, roving black eyes, and a crooked smile. *Une femme fatale* down to her well-turned ankles.

"I'll bet that's Vera," he remarked.

Mercado nodded abstractedly. He had not only picked Vera from the group but had noted the pretty childlike face of one whom they were to know as Cléopâtre. She had attracted his attention because her naïveté contrasted with the boldness of the others. Not that she lacked self-possession, but it was latent. She evidently did not want to be looked at, but moved with lowered eyes, so quietly.

"What do you think she is doing here?" Mercado asked. "Her prettiness is not heightened by her costume. She belongs under the open sky." Probably this observation, which turned out to be so accurate, was induced by her healthy coloring and lack of make-up.

The advent of the Russians intensified the spirit of revelry. After a few drinks, Halsey reflected, Americans share this propensity. He imagined a Russian, in good condition, could start a riot on a desert isle. At any rate this group never failed, and he observed them many an evening, to give the illusion of having a gorgeous time. Their laughter was always spontaneous, their dancing full of zest. The two professors were by then in a most appreciative humor. Their monastic campus might, for all it mattered, have been known to them only in a previous incarnation.

Mercado was better equipped for the place than Halsey. That is, his French, though none too perfect, was more fluent, and he danced exceedingly well. Before long he was buffeting the swaying throng with the lovely black-eyed enchantress in his arms. He led her back to the bar and introduced her. She suggested they should sit at a table. She had a friend . . .

Halsey disliked the friend on first sight but she improved over the champagne. Her name was Liza. *La femme fatale* turned out, as expected, to be Vera.

"Do you know a chap called Hamilton Corey?" Mercado asked when the wine had established an illusion of intimacy between the four of them.

"Hamilton!" Her smile was ravishing. "I love Hamilton. But what has become of him? I have not seen him for nearly a week. And he promised . . . but you Americans, you do not understand friendship."

"And what do you mean by that?" asked Mercado, delighted at the turn the conversation had taken. He was feeling that their trip to Europe was going to be a success after all.

"You give yourself up to your feelings for a night, just as we do. You drink, make love, gamble like true Russians. But the morning after you are so different. When we start something we carry it through, not caring where it may take us. There is always time to reflect afterwards. But you, you check yourselves. You ask questions. You suspect. You analyze motives. I would hate to wake up like an American."

"Evidently," Mercado said, "you have waked up with an American."

"There you are," she replied, "no Russian would make such a remark . . . now."

Laughingly they drank each other's health. The lights were lowered. The smallest *danseuse* took the floor.

"You must watch," Vera announced, and they stood up at the table in order to see. "She is very good. *C'est une danse Juive.*" It looked to them like any other peasant dance..

"I didn't know there was such a thing," Mercado remarked. "But she's a Russian, isn't she?"

"Of course," Vera whispered.

They opened another bottle. The service at the Caveau was far too efficient. They didn't have to ask for champagne, automatically a full bottle seemed to replace the empty one in the

ice pail. An unwelcome thought suddenly
checked Mercado. He turned to Halsey and
asked him how much money he had. Three
hundred francs, the latter replied after
a careful count, for he had had five hundred
when he entered. "It isn't enough," Mercado
said, "it may not even cover the check and I've
asked them out to breakfast."

"And they call New York expensive!"
Halsey groaned.

Vera must have caught from his expression
a suspicion of what was wrong.

"*Qu'est ce que c'est?*" she asked.

Mercado told her of their difficulty.

"But I have money," she said, "you can give
it back to me to-morrow."

Though Halsey realized that most Europeans believe the pockets of Americans are automatically refilled with dollars over night, her
offer startled him by its spontaneity. He had
been attracted from the beginning by Vera's
full-blooded voluptuousness. She was not at
all his type, that is, she did not resemble the
conspicuously well bred woman to whom he
had always been drawn in the past. He had
never had any use for the more instinctive tem-

peraments in whom emotion tends to be hysterical. They had always seemed a little common, even vulgar. At home reserve is such a fundamental attribute of breeding.

Vera, owing to her foreign tongue and Continental manners, or because she really was of good family as her title, if genuine, would indicate, combined, he felt, passionate intensity with those esthetic qualities which one expects to find only in the progeny of several sheltered generations. At any rate he was so attracted by Vera that he was conscious of envying Mercado who, by his initial advance, had acquired prior rights. And Liza, who resembled Vera in many ways, was such a diluted substitute.

He admitted to himself that the thrill he received on meeting her eyes may have had more to do with his feelings than the plausible reasons which his intellect provided. It is so difficult not to rationalize.

When her generous offer substantiated the philosophy of impulse which he had heard her expound with amusement—he had thought it but a line which she handed out indiscriminately as a matter of policy—his liking for her was transferred to another plane. He became really interested. Here was some one who lived as the spirit moved her and not as her bank book or the social register dictated. He recalled what Mercado had said on the way over about Russians, and began to take the adventure more seriously. Did her offer not prove that she liked them, or at least Mercado—his second thought gave him no pleasure—and that when she liked . . .

But could they accept her money? Would a Russian hesitate? He was inclined to take her at her word.

"What about it, John?" Halsey asked in English.

"First let's see where we stand," Mercado replied, apparently not much concerned. "I'll obtain the data from our hostess." He got up and left the table.

Halsey thought it strange that Mercado was taking their new friends so casually. He usually analyzed every remark, gesture, slip of the tongue, to a degree that was irritating. For this once he had let himself go, buoyed up by the wine, and was drifting gayly along, relishing each moment as it passed. Vera's offer, he assured Halsey afterwards, had at the time

seemed quite natural. His hesitation about accepting it was only caused by the fear that the
amount needed might turn out to be too much.
He left them, swaying slightly, for he had the
sensation of walking on air, exhilarated by
Vera's responsiveness. "The one infallible in-
toxicant," Mercado always insisted, "is a pretty
woman's admiration. It is more dangerous than
alcohol. The hang-over is so demoralizing.
And yet I never have the strength to resist it."

No one said anything after he departed.
Halsey tried, desperately, to come out of his
shell and make what personality he had, mani-
fest. But the force of his desire effectually tied
his tongue. They sat, the three of them, stiffly,
and pretended to watch the dancers. Halsey
looked at his watch. It was four o'clock.

*"Tiens!"* exclaimed Vera, "I'm so glad."

Hamilton, beaming all over, was dodging
the couples as he crossed the floor. He was
evidently pleased to find his friends together.

"I've broken away," he shouted in high
spirits, "these last nights have been something
terrible. I sail to-day."

Vera and Liza fell on him bodily. He was
made to sit between them. The inexhaustible

ice pail was despoiled once more of its virgin bottle. Vera berated him gently for his neglect. Halsey might just as well have been asleep for all the notice that was taken of him.

Mercado returned. Hamilton was delighted to see him. Vera didn't bother even to look his way. Halsey felt better now that he had a companion in exile.

"From now on it's my party," Hamilton managed to interpolate between his responses to the flattering effusions with which he was being deluged from both sides.

It was.

They made the acquaintance of Konyaks and ate quantities of caviar while another bottle of wine completed the severance of their sensations from reality. They sat in a long oblong box, between a tapestried wall and a long low table. Some one strummed a balalaika. Now and again one or more of the guests burst into song or executed a grotesque dance, unperturbed by the boy, who had to shove by, in order to pass with his tray of refreshments. The smoke formed arabesques beneath the stenciled ceil-

ing. An American came in with a glimmer of
dawn, which the swinging door immediately
evicted, and made them a speech of apology.
Beastly, was it not, that he and his like had
followed them even here, with their bourgeois
sightseeing faces and Western twangs. No
place was sacred any more from their prying
curiosity. He was profoundly sorry. He
begged their indulgence. Mercado, though annoyed by self-consciousness, so typically American, tried to comfort him. Halsey felt quite
set up to be taken for an habitué even though
he knew the credit belonged to his esoteric
companions.

The five then rode in a taxi through the Bois
de Boulogne. While the two women competed
for Hamilton's caresses, Halsey considered the
trees and flowers which looked artificial in their
somnolent quiescence. The air felt clean in
his lungs and he gratefully accepted the stray
caresses of Vera in far too beatific a mood even
to consider the humility of his rôle. Mercado,
on one of the two little seats in front, sat with
rigid academic disapproval, looking straight
ahead, pretending to ignore his companions.

Halsey tried to bring him back from time to time but he curtly repelled all advances. His austerity, at such an hour, was deemed none too friendly. Halsey eventually left him to his thoughts.

By nine o'clock they were sitting in some café, the sunlight pouring in through the open doors and windows, drinking *fine*. Hamilton waved aside his two ardent admirers and tried to talk seriously. He would not see the professors again until their return to America and he wanted to give them his address.

Mercado insisted on sharing the expenses of the night. This was not easy to arrange as he had no money with him. And there was also the problem of getting the women home. Neither girl wanted to leave Hamilton. At ten o'clock a scheme was adopted by the majority. Hamilton was to take Liza home first. Afterwards he was to escort Vera to her domicile. Finally he would go to the bank where Mercado had his money, and replenish his wallet. The boat train left at one. Liza's, the only dissenting voice, was by this time none too strong. She preferred to be taken home last which, after looking at Vera, Halsey felt was bad judgment on her part.    Eventually she was overruled.

Mercado and Halsey sat like mummies over their empty glasses while Hamilton went about his errands.    They made several bets as to whether or not he would catch his boat.    Mercado thought he would.

At half-past ten Hamilton returned and left with Vera.    Halsey raised the odds.

Suddenly Mercado began to explain the reason for his surliness in the cab.    He claimed the fresh air had sobered him so that the others looked repulsive in the morning light with their midnight countenances.    Halsey was inclined to think that his vanity had been wounded by Vera's desertion.    He made a mild suggestion to this effect.    Mercado denied it vehemently.

"I thought," he said, "you knew me better." Mercado pretended to be hurt.

At eleven-thirty Hamilton came back alone, looking a bit bedraggled, but cheerful as ever. He thanked them for their patience and wanted to buy another drink.    Halsey should, for financial reasons, have encouraged him, but his New England conscience restrained him.    They put Hamilton in a taxi at twelve o'clock and directed the driver to his flat. They returned to their hotel and beds.

Hamilton did not catch the boat. He wired Mercado for additional funds to enable him to take a later one. He has not yet returned the loan.

## CHAPTER TWO

"HOW would you like," Mercado suggested as they were finishing their second breakfast just twelve hours after their usual time, "to pay one more visit to the Caveau before starting on our excursion?"

"It suits me," Halsey replied, "but feeling as you do toward Vera, I don't see why you ever want to see her again."

Mercado had been fulminating against Vera before they had gone downstairs. He had grudgingly admitted her magnetism, which he defined as sex appeal, but had denied her any other good quality. Halsey, on the contrary, had asserted that her attitude of the night before was not only natural but to her credit. Hamilton was an old friend. They were new acquaintances. Only if she had deserted Hamilton for them, which obviously was to her interest as he was leaving the country, would they have the right to condemn her as a hypocritical schemer on the look-out for the main chance.

"But she switches her affection," Mercado had claimed, "as we turn on a water tap. It means nothing. It's merely technique and I've no use for artificial emotion."

"In the first place you exaggerate," Halsey had rejoined. "You overlook the fact that she had been drinking." And he pointed out that even if the justice of his observation were granted, it made no difference. Vera had *métier*, more of it than any woman he had ever known. By it she gave him pleasure. He enjoyed her company as he had enjoyed nothing else in Europe. Why should he ask for more? He didn't plan to marry her.

"*Métier!*" Mercado snapped back. "I think you misuse the word. I am willing to grant her *métier*, the *métier* of a prostitute, but it doesn't interest me."

Halsey suppressed the annoyance which Mercado's crude designation had provoked and replied that great skill always delighted him. He was eclectic enough in his tastes to enjoy both the antics of Babe Ruth and the painting of Pablo Picasso. Vera translated her superabundant energy into a form of expression which they were taught, as respectable members of society, to deprecate. But what of it? He was not concerned with her morals.

Mercado had not been convinced. He asserted that art must be sincere and that her art was hypocritical. She served up emotions which were meaningless for they were but replicas or imitations of the genuine emotions she must once have felt for some one else.

"And what else does any interpretative artist do?" Halsey had demanded, pleased that his argument had such a rational defense. "Do you think the violinist, who brings ecstasy to his audience, is utilizing his own imagination? Is he not frankly borrowing the emotion of some great composer and animating it by his own genius?"

Silenced by this reasoning, Mercado could only grunt, "You can have her," and had started to get out of bed. Halsey was in good humor, for he rarely left the field with honor after a debate with his friend. He suspected his victory was owing to the fact that Mercado knew, in his heart, that piqued vanity was responsible for his distaste. They had dressed and had gone down to the restaurant without further discussion. Halsey felt shaky but very well considering the amount of liquor he had consumed.

It was then that Mercado astonished him by suggesting another visit to the Caveau. Halsey had already put it out of his mind, for he was too diffident to go there alone and, besides, was eagerly looking forward to their trip.

"We'll never get off on bicycles," he said, "if we go in for Paris night life."

"I thought you were anxious to see Vera again?"

"I am, but I'd like to know what you expect to get out of it."

"I liked the place and I want to find out if such a night can be repeated."

"Bosh!" Halsey said.

Mercado laughed and called him a good-natured don. No wonder the boys liked him. Of course he had something else in mind. "Do you remember," he asked, "that young looking face I pointed out, with the large blue eyes? I met her later as I was coming off the floor with Liza. We nearly ran into each other. As we stood, hesitating which way to pass, our eyes met. Hers are really magnificent. Blue, with little black dancing points. We both smiled. I felt as if we knew each other very well." And he went on to say that she, though not as obviously fascinating as Vera, or even very beautiful, was, he thought, a person. He wanted to know her. He did not think she was spoiled, as yet, by the life. As Halsey liked Vera, both of them should be satisfied.

"I'm game," Halsey answered and they wandered over to the Dome for company and a liqueur with which to pass the intervening hours.

The Caveau was as stimulating as on the previous night. They watched the performers, drank and danced with even greater gusto, feeling as much at home as if they belonged to the establishment. A large party of English people occupied the end table, some of whom were always drifting over to the bar where they amused them by the strangeness of their clichés. Halsey observed that the American language, as it is spoken, had strayed farther from the mother tongue than the literary idiom. But that, of course, was to be expected.

[ 42 ]

While part of his mind was pleasantly chatting with these chance acquaintances, another part was asking the time, wondering how soon Vera would come upstairs, worrying whether she would still be amiable, and prefiguring the attitude Mercado would take toward her. He hoped Mercado would not forget his resentment and renew his friendship. He feared he would be rude and spoil his own chances of becoming intimate. All in all he had plenty to think about while he automatically carried on a casual conversation with a British monocle.

Though he thought the entrance door was never out of his sight, he must have lost it for several minutes, as he was first aware of Vera's arrival when joyously greeted from behind. She and Liza, smiling welcome, ran up to them at the bar, routing the English by their precipitous advent. They seemed quite unconscious that their conduct, the previous evening, had been unusual, and made no other comment on the night that had passed than to express comic horror at their condition. They pretended to remember nothing of what had occurred after four o'clock, a most convenient lapse practiced, Mercado remarked, by women who enjoyed the small hours. Halsey wondered where his friend had obtained this bit of wisdom.

Halsey feared, for a moment, that the spirits of the Russians would be dashed by the coldness of Mercado's reception. He misconstrued their character. Liza suggested a table. Halsey assented quickly, getting a black look from Mercado, but he wasn't going to let his friend spoil his pleasure after having been persuaded to revisit the Caveau contrary to his wishes. Mercado's objections, he learned afterwards, were based on other grounds than he had thought.

Vera asked Mercado to dance. Halsey thought he was going to refuse but he didn't.

When they were walking back toward the table, Vera suddenly swung round and faced him.

"Are you through with me?" she asked, just like that, with no preface or explanation.

"Yes," Mercado answered, "I don't care to be made a fool of twice."

"*Vous êtes drôle,*" she said. "Some day you will understand us better. Let it be as you wish." And she calmly turned away. Mercado felt he had been hasty but fortified himself by the thought that after all he hadn't returned to see Vera, and Halsey had. At least so he told Halsey.

The foursome was getting on pretty well considering that Mercado took no part in the conversation. Halsey felt that he leaned too much on his friend and would pick up the language much faster if he went out more alone. He even began to forget that half his phrases were incorrect and actually told several anecdotes of American college life in his halting vernacular. He talked directly to Vera, disregarding Liza, who had a mild bovine disposition, and didn't seem to care. Mercado pretended to listen but his expression showed his thoughts were elsewhere.

After a bottle of wine and several dances he excused himself. When next Halsey noticed him he was dancing with the Russian girl whom he had pointed out the evening before. She was shorter than Halsey had thought, but strong looking. Her clear complexion was conspicuous in that atmosphere, though the professionals seemed to stand the life better than the majority of their guests.

[ 45 ]

Mercado had found her sitting alone in the corridor set aside for the entertainers. She was gazing into the room, regarding, he felt, some far-away scene which bore no relation to the frivolous roistering which was taking place before her. Mercado had the impression that her spirit was longing for vast open steppes, wild horses, and the wind that has crossed a continent. He stood before her looking at her hands, nearly forgetting to speak because of her hands. They startled him for they exhibited to an even greater degree that curious contrast of opposites which had first attracted his attention. They were broad, strong, efficient. Each individual muscle, on each individual finger, had that completeness of form which results from full development. Yet the skin was white and soft, and her finger nails were long, polished and tinted like the nails of those French women who concentrate all their thought on their physical seductiveness.

"Will you dance with me?" he asked, leaning over slightly, one hand on the table.

"Yes," she said, "I have been waiting for you." And her answer did not sound at all strange.

[ 46 ]

The dance was disappointing. She could not follow Mercado's American steps. He was what is sometimes called, incorrectly, a temperamental dancer. That is, his movements interpreted the music and varied according as the music varied. His partner had to be sensitive both to the rhythm and to the slightest pressure of his body. They got along badly, as Cléopâtre—she told him her name was Clara but that her friends always called her Cléopâtre—had only an elementary knowledge of ballroom technique though she claimed to have given peasant dances professionally. Mercado was much upset; he wished to make an impression. She was not perturbed but coolly remarked that with a little practice she would do better. Cléopâtre did not realize that their uncoördinated movements were extremely disagreeable to Mercado, who considered dancing a torture when it was not a delight.

After the music ceased they stood for a moment, side by side. "I am unhappy," she said. "I do not like this life. It is only my first week here."

"You'll like it better when you have become accustomed to it."

"No," she answered with heat. "I will hate it the more. It is not for me, this play, this travesty. Not after what I've seen. I do it to support my son who is in the country. I hate it."

Her eyes flashed. The bitter phrase, *"Je le deteste"* shocked him. Her virulence was unexpected, for her features were those of a pretty girl, naïve and doll-like. He could hardly believe she had borne a son.

"You are young," he said, "to be a mother."

She looked up at him, bending her head to one side. A shy quizzical smile flitted, like the dive of a martin, across her face. She said nothing. Mercado, fascinated by her volatility, invited her to come and sit at his table. Vera and Liza exchanged glances at their approach. Halsey rose to greet them. Everybody shook hands. The thought occurred to Halsey that there would be no more dancing unless one woman was left to sit alone. He did not know what was in the minds of the others but a heavy silence descended upon the company. Not even the toast, bottoms up, which seemed to be the custom among Russians even when champagne

[ 48 ]

was the beverage, lightened the oppression. He felt sorry for Liza.

Mercado had assumed the enigmatic smile which is so feared by his pupils and sat tapping the stem of his glass with his index finger. Something had to happen and Halsey was unable to interfere. His French had completely deserted him. He couldn't get out a word.

Suddenly Vera started to talk in Russian. The sounds gushed forth like water from a hydraulic ram. Her eyes burned. Her gestures had the dynamic quality of a great emotional actress. The professors could not understand a word. At the slightest let-up Liza joined in, her voice pitched an octave higher. Halsey felt as if every one must be looking at their table. A glance around reassured him. In that room more than an emphatic voice was needed to attract attention. He turned to Cléopâtre.

Her lashes rested peacefully on her cheeks. Not even her color had risen. When Vera paused, she opened her eyes, looked candidly into Vera's, and softly drawled a few words as if she were commenting on the weather. The result was a storm that made the previous deluge seem, in comparison, insignificant. Yet the voices were sufficiently restrained to keep within the bounds of propriety. Halsey wanted to get away. Mercado said afterwards that he had enjoyed it but his friend did not believe him. Mercado, he felt, had, like everybody else, his affectations.

Vera's impetuous attack continued unabated, until Halsey feared it was never going to end, but eventually a decision was reached for the fury ebbed as suddenly as it had risen. The three women were instantaneously all smiles and amiability. Cléopâtre calmly drained her glass, then carefully rose and excused herself. Evidently she had been vanquished but was leaving the fray with every honor, for she alone had not allowed one hair to be ruffled.

Her firmness astonished Halsey. The violent verbal onslaught of the two mature women had not perturbed, in the least, her infantile gravity.

Mercado jumped to his feet. Cléopâtre drew him aside and thanked him prettily in broken English. Her accent was delightful. Mercado explains that something about the way she rolled the "r" in "very" must have struck a sympathetic chord in him, for quite on impulse, without the idea having occurred to him previously, he asked her to dine with him on the following night.

She would meet him, she replied, at the Rotonde in Montparnasse at six o'clock. Did he know that quarter?

Mercado knew it well, far too well he realized a moment later, but assented of course. Then he returned to the others. He was troubled, he told Halsey in English, by two things. In the first place he felt he had been disloyal, for he had suggested the bicycle trip and now had postponed it again without asking his friend's consent. Halsey told him that was quite all right. He would go out with Vera if she were willing. Secondly he knew a great many people in the quarter. He wondered, if his escapade were reported back home, would his reputation suffer and hurt his chances for advancement. Halsey tried to reassure him, asserting that no one would imagine the child-like Cléopâtre was improper company for a serious college professor. "Doubtless they will think you are showing the sights of the city to one of your pupils," he suggested. Mercado

[ 51 ]

gave him a fishy look out of his left eye. It is true, Cléopâtre would never be taken for an American but, on the other hand, it would indeed be a sad state of affairs if a university career restricted friendship to one's own country-women. "And Cléopâtre," Halsey concluded, "looks respectable enough to go anywhere."

"We haven't seen her in street clothes," Mercado objected, but Halsey knew his assurances had made him feel better.

Everything seemed satisfactorily arranged when Liza, the mild phlegmatic Liza, who must have been stewing over the injustice that had been done her, took advantage of a chance inquiry, to hurl a grenade that nearly upset the arrangement. As a result the two professors sat for the second time in a café until the sun recalled their sense of humor by flashing its smile on their evening shirt fronts.

Halsey did not believe one word Liza had said. Mercado didn't know, he was more than half inclined to credit her statements. He had felt from the beginning that there was something anomalous about Cléopâtre, something that set her apart from other women. Liza's account of her past activities would be, if true, a plausible solution of the mystery.

Halsey contended that the account was absurd on the face of it. That Liza, having been callously neglected and snubbed—his New England conscience exaggerated the offense and Mercado was nearer the truth in considering their action only a matter of course—and having drunk sufficient wine to lose her restraint, would naturally amplify any bit of gossip into the most lurid tale her mind was capable of imagining. "Why," he said, "you've looked at Cléopâtre. Faces lie but if her candid, girlish smile and her open regard conceal the villainies which Liza ascribes to her, that face is the most stupendous liar this world has ever known. The thought alone is monstrous."

"You forget, my dear colleague," Mercado sarcastically rejoined, "Cléopâtre is not an American flapper."

Halsey had an inkling then of the complex twist in his friend's character which was to carry him into an adventure which might have ended tragically. He knew from the way Mercado spoke that he would be only too pleased if Cléopâtre was everything that Liza had claimed.

And the question, which had released her invective, was so innocent. Vera had been describing her wanderings. After her escape she had lived in Constantinople, Rome and Nice, arriving finally at Paris where she planned to remain. That is, until the present régime was overthrown. She, like all the others, still considered this imminent. Their information, derived from prejudiced sources, was so untrustworthy one would think they had been reading the American papers. She told them about the life she had formerly led on her husband's estate near Moscow. It had not differed greatly from that described in Tolstoy's novels. Without thinking Mercado asked: "What was Cléopâtre during the years of turmoil? She must have been hardly more than a child."

Then Liza began to speak, calmly enough. Clara was not what she seemed. One need only mention her name. There was no Russian who had not heard of her exploits and of her cruelty.

Vera had interrupted to add: "And of her courage. Don't forget she was fighting for us."

"Yes," Liza had continued. "Her name, her real name, not that silly affectation which she so delights in, is said to be enough to throw a

Bolshevik child into a fit of terror. She is the *croquemitaine* of the Caucasus." And she went on to tell about one town which was supposed to have given up a couple of stragglers to the Bolsheviks. The regiment, to which Clara was attached, captured it a few months later without a struggle. A council of war was called to decide what punishment should be inflicted. After the various officers had spoken Clara Demidoff got up and derided them for their effeminate weakness, asserting that an example must be made that would strike terror into the countryside, or their future operations would be imperiled. Ashamed of being outdone by a girl, the council was converted to her point of view. Having herded the inhabitants in the square, the males, down to the suckling infants, were passed in line, and their hands were hacked off by sabers before the eyes of their wives and mothers. As a result the whole community slowly died of starvation. "Yes," Liza shrilled, "she is renowned among Russians. Her arms have been bathed to the elbow in blood. Her fingers know the feel of gouging a living eye from its socket. She is supposed to have done wonderful things. You can ask any Russian."

Vera interrupted again. They relapsed into their own language and argued with such heat that it was a long while before the professors were able to join the conversation. Vera whispered to Halsey that Liza was not a true Russian but was tainted with sentimentality. At any rate, the spirit of enjoyment had been dissipated and Halsey and Mercado took the first opportunity to leave their companions and retire to a café.

## CHAPTER THREE

"DON'T you really think," Mercado abruptly demanded at breakfast, "that they're a pair of vulgar charlatans masquerading under false names in order to separate innocent Americans from their dollars?"

"What pair?" asked Halsey, knowing whom he meant but annoyed that Mercado should except Cléopâtre.

"Vera and Liza."

"I do not." He decided to disregard the omission. Doubtless the women were not spending their nights at a cabaret in order to amuse themselves but he felt sure they were in no sense professional adventuresses. Outside circumstances had forced them into this mode of life.

Mercado did not agree with him. He insisted that they would have torn out each other's hair before them if they had not realized it

[ 57 ]

would have cost them their jobs. Did not Halsey remember what Vera had said about the cigarette girl? That she did not dare refuse her, even though the price of the cigarettes was exorbitant, for fear she would be reported to the management.

"Which only goes to prove," Halsey rejoined, "her essential decency. She was tipping us off so that we could turn the girl down ourselves."

Mercado began to laugh. He put his arm on Halsey's shoulder and asked him if he was in love with Vera.

"I am not." Halsey answered with emphasis. Direct questions were difficult for him. When he attempted evasion, he could not help implying there was something he wanted to conceal, while an honest answer was likely to be embarrassing. This time he tried to give the impression of complete candor. "She attracts me. She interests me. I enjoy being with her. But, though I cannot qualify as an expert on sentimental attachments, I am sufficiently experienced to guarantee that my feeling for Vera is in nowise such a major passion as the word love connotes."

"Come down to earth, Bill."

Mercado impatiently walked to the window. He wanted, Halsey imagined, to talk about Cléopâtre but they had gone over her character at such length the night before that he probably felt the subject was pretty well exhausted.

Turning suddenly, after pausing for some seconds with his back to the room, he astonished Halsey by saying: "I've made up my mind. We're making fools of ourselves. Let's give up these women and get started on our trip. We came over to see something of Europe, not to indulge our appetites."

Halsey hesitated. He was sufficiently familiar with Mercado's uneven disposition not to be astonished by a sudden shift of mood. He judged that John was offering to renounce Cléopâtre because some trifle had upset him. If he took him at his word, Mercado would no doubt live up to the bargain, but would be filled with self-commiseration and regret during the whole of their excursion. What he really wanted was to be convinced, as if against his will, that there was no point in so drastic a retraction. Halsey considered it wiser to play up to this unexpressed desire. At least such is the reason he admitted to himself. Probably the pleasure he took in Vera had more to do with his decision than he knew.

"What's the matter now?" he asked in order to bring the grievance into the open.

"Only what I said. I was repelled by the sordid clash of the women."

Halsey pointed out that considering the intensity of their fury they had all acted up very well. In fact, Vera's self-control had filled him with admiration. He would never have believed a woman could express such dynamic vehemence by such economical means. Besides, Mercado should remember that last night he himself had professed to have enjoyed the performance.

After allowing a few seconds for his remarks to sink in, Halsey asked, with apparent ingenuousness: "Why don't you go out with Cléopâtre alone? Surely you should be able to discover if she's on the level by having her to yourself for some hours."

"Not a bad idea!" Mercado muttered, proving to his friend's satisfaction that this had been his intention in the first place. "Meanwhile you can undertake the scientific investigation of Vera's morals."

"A pleasant enough prospect," Halsey agreed.

"But," Mercado added, "don't make a fool of yourself by falling in love with her. I feel responsible, having persuaded you to take this vacation."

Halsey reflected that in life each individual sees those qualities in his friends which he himself possesses. Thus the cheat is always discovering he is being cheated, the miser complains of the parsimony of his associates, and the idealist gives praise for the goodness of humanity. Mercado, apprehensive that Cléopâtre should sweep him farther than his scheme of life sanctioned, evaded the warnings of his consciousness by transferring his own fear to Halsey, who took the caution lightly.

They parted good-humoredly at five o'clock and did not see each other until the following day.

Halsey was unable to meet Vera until she reported at the Caveau to make ready for the evening. He occupied himself during the interval by strolling through the old quarter, near the cathedral of Notre Dame. Then he made his way back to the Dingo, a small bar that had been taken up by the Americans of the quarter. There he met Harold Stearns and discussed the effects of prohibition on the younger intellectuals. They were interrupted by Fannie, renowned for her conviviality, who had two sailors and an English poet in her train. Some one started pounding out a popular tune on the piano. Halsey left for Montmartre.

The time passed pleasantly. After a cordial welcome by Vera, Halsey was quite content to sip his *fine à l'eau* and dance an occasional number. He was relieved that no dramatic scene disrupted his incandescent mood. To sun himself in the aureole of Vera's magnetism was enough for him. Also, his French was improving, though not so fast as Vera's English. She would, he calculated, speak his language fluently, long before he acquired her foster tongue.

Cléopâtre's arrival without Mercado aroused Halsey's curiosity. He invited her to dance. "What," he asked, "have you done with my friend?"

"He is *très gentil, ce Monsieur*. I like him very much."

"But what have you done with him?"

"We took a walk and then had dinner. He was very kind and took me here. He did not want to come inside, he said, to-night."

Halsey wondered if anything lay behind her simple statements. Could such candor be real? Or was it a screen hiding a complex nature? He began to understand why Mercado found her attractive.

Meanwhile Vera was only able to give him part of her attention. She would sit down for ten minutes. Bewitched by her voice, expressive eyes and hands, he would lose all sense of time, when suddenly she would say: "I must go back now," and disappear down the stairs to take up again those mysterious duties in the lower regions.

Halsey did not care. He had drunk so many brandies and sodas that all count was lost. Eventually he hardly knew if Vera was with him or if he was alone.

Undoubtedly she was there when he noticed Mrs. Horace P. Smith sitting at a table nearby. He couldn't be mistaken. The same high collar, the same puffy eyes, the yellow lifeless skin, the hair drawn back from her forehead into a tight bun. Mrs. Horace P. Smith, the Dean's wife. One attended her teas as one attended church on Easter day, to discharge a duty to society. She was a symbol, like a wax statue of the Virgin. Had she noticed him? Would it be better to ignore her, or to pay her a short visit? What the devil, he was sober. "Excuse—*excusez-moi*, Vera. Old friend across the room. Just a minute, *certainement!*"

He lurched to the other table, gripped the back of a chair. His body insisted on rocking back and forth. He gripped till the tendons stood out and the knuckles turned white, but of course, she wouldn't notice.

"Mrs. Smith. What a great, an unexpected pleasure! Dean Smith should have announced your arrival. Seeing the other side of life, I suppose. This atmosphere" (waving an unsteady hand), "this smoke and music is, ah, quaint, don't you find? Fancy meeting you here! Like a breath of, ah, country air from Greensborough!"

She made no answer. He looked down at her hands, resting primly on the edge of the

[ 64 ]

table.  Curious hands for a Dean's wife . . .
and why hadn't he noticed them before?  So
many rings.  Why didn't she ask him to sit
down?  He cleared his throat:

"I came here because of an old friend of
mine, an exiled countess whom I met in Chi-
cago before the war" (that was a lie).  "Her es-
tates, thousands of acres, all confiscated, and
here she is, bravely earning her living.  A very
interesting life, she tells me, but very tiring.
I do hope to see something of you before you
sail for the States."

Why didn't she reply?  Was she going to
cut him dead.  Twelve years of sober effort on
the Faculty, and this was the end.  Well, he'd
try to tell her something, make her see the other
side of it.  He didn't care, now.

"Greensborough, teaching nice young boys
to enjoy Keats a little, attending your interesting teas, all that . . . you understand, of
course, Mrs. Smith, that it's only one side of
life.  Apollonianism.  We have a deep, ingrained, primitive desire for the orgy.  Dionysus.  Pressing the purple grapes.  Worship of
Cybele.  Sacrifices, degradation of the self,
torchlight processions.  Maypole dances in a

Christian country. I called for madder music, stronger wine. Burning niggers for crimes we'd like to perform. You understand, Mrs. Smith.

"And then, back in Greensborough, the other side of the medal, the calm Apollonian friezes, freeze, frozen, with laurel wreaths and . . . 'what we principally enjoy in Wordsworth is his appeal to the better side of our natures.' No hint of buried frenzies, all calm, Professor Halsey of the Norton Chair of English Letters. You understand, Mrs. Smith.

"But even in the orgy, there are certain points I can't pass. Don't know why, nothing intellectual, Puritan background, university training . . . women, I never . . . well, I can't explain, but you'll understand, Mrs. Smith. Something keeps me from yielding on that one point. If I did, everything would crumble away, professorship, gone, Apollonian calm, gone, your charming teas, gone, gone, but I won't surrender. Tell me that you understand, this once, when we can be perfectly frank . . ."

"*Dis-donc, toi. Je m'en fous de ton anglais. Oui ou non, veux tu coucher avec moi?*"

Her voice cut through the film of smoke.

For the first time he looked at her face, and as he watched it, her features changed into those of a hard, cold, nasty French cocotte.

"My mistake," he muttered. *"Pardonnez-moi.* Thought you were Mrs. Smith."

He stumbled away, but a waiter stopped him to ask whether he wasn't going to pay for the lady's drink. All right, surely he would, in the reckoning for the next table. But where was Vera? He waited patiently, but Vera did not return. Perhaps she would never speak to him again. And of course, he couldn't leave to-morrow night without seeing her. Mercado would have to wait or go alone. He'd speak to Mercado. . . . And he paid his bill and stumbled to a taxi.

As it turned out, he had no difficulty on that score.

Mercado, on leaving the hotel, had gone immediately to the Rotonde. He chose a table on the terrace ahead of time so as to avoid the embarrassment of finding himself next to acquaintances. He waited patiently enough until the appointed hour and nervously during the subsequent thirty minutes. The practice of being late, he reflected, was an irritating though effective stratagem. Those American girls, who dispense with such traditional wiles, throw away one of the most potent weapons in the feminine armory. The sensation of waiting, while the fear that the expected party may not be coming grows increasingly acute, is likely to undermine the sturdiest masculine morale. Though in the beginning he did not care much whether Cléopâtre arrived or not, in the end he was scrutinizing each figure that issued from the Metro, each taxi that turned the corner from Boulevard Raspail, each pedestrian that loomed into view down the long stretch of Boulevard Montparnasse. Finally Cléopâtre emerged from the shadow of the subway entrance and glided up to him, her gloved hand extended, a casual apology on her lips. His spirits fell abruptly. Her coming was an anticlimax; only a goddess could have justified his agitation, and Cléopâtre seemed complacently bourgeois. Her voice should have trembled with eagerness. Her eyes should have glittered with delight.

They had coffee together. They watched, as if they had never noticed it before, the *garçon* pouring oppositely colored liquids from shining

tin pitchers. They did not know what to talk
about.

"It is hot," she said, "in the Metro."

"You should try our New York subways,"
he replied.

From time to time his eyes, straying over to
the Dome, distinguished friends among the
changing multitude. He mused upon the rest-
lessness of Americans. Now the Dome had
their patronage. Two years before it had been
the Rotonde.

The Rotonde, he reflected, looks across the
boulevard at the Dome as Scylla upon Charyb-
dis. Though the appetites of the rival cafés are
equally voracious, their tastes are incompatible.
Long ago the Dome, at that time unpretentious,
went in for cochers and bluesmocked laborers.
The Rotonde specialized in conspirators. Trot-
sky himself is supposed to have initiated his far-
reaching plots behind its discreet portals.
American men of position hesitated before being seen too often in either. Their women
passed quickly by, holding their breath, their
eyes averted.

Yet, even in those early days before the war

a group of seasoned veterans, who made Paris their home, maintained a continuous poker game in the back room of the Dome. One could watch them scrutinizing hands which puzzled many a novice, for the French government prefers that playing cards should have no numbers on their corners, while dawn and a trolley car came rattling down the Boulevard Montparnasse.

On a fair June day in 1920 the Rotonde cocooned itself behind boards to emerge, months later, several times enlarged, its garish walls strewn with postimpressionistic paintings. An upper floor had been incorporated. It became the thing for Americans to sun themselves upon its terrace and to dance the night away before esoteric pictures to the music of home-brewed jazz. . . .

"I like this quarter," Cléopâtre said. "Have you a cigarette? So many Russian artists."

"I smoke a pipe but we can send for some," he answered, recalling that the next mutation was more gradual. First the more seasoned quarterites began to shrug their shoulders, *à la française*, lisping, in the English manner: "But one doesn't go there any more. The crowd is just too awful. The Dome is really pleasanter." In a little while only the late arrivals from home sipped their Amer-Picon at the more luxuriant café. The Dome became the accepted meeting place of emancipated America. Its terrace was conspicuous for hatless females who are not, technically, what the Parisian thinks they are, shapely ankles and informal costumes. Meanwhile the Rotonde suffered no loss in popularity, but merely an altered complexion. Its new devotees were drawn from every nation; even an occasional Frenchman, with a flair for the exotic, honored the management by his attendance. For the most part strange types from Egypt or the Balkans, Swiss, South Americans, two Hindoos (one in a tall turban), an American negress, three Japanese artists, many Swedes, Danes and Norwegians, a sprinkling of Germans, Hungarians, Italians, Spaniards, Greeks and last, most numerous of all, the Russians. . . .

"I come here nearly every afternoon to meet my friends," she said, breaking in upon his thoughts.

"And I the same, but we Americans meet across the street."

"It is original," she said.

"*Oui, c'est original.*" Mercado assented though somewhat puzzled as to what she meant.

"I like," she added, "to walk in the garden of the Luxembourg. Would it please you to go there with me now?"

"It would please me very much," he replied, astonished at the turn their afternoon was taking. He had not bargained for such a recreation, though he would have been hard put to say what he had bargained for.

"But won't you have a drink of something stronger before we set off?"

"No," she said, "I do not like to drink."

Mercado wondered, as they strolled toward the entrance of the park, whether he could take her statement literally. He wondered more when, having passed the gate, she pointed out flowers, statues, vistas, which she loved, to him who twelve years before had made rather a fetish of walking in the garden and had never visited it since.

She loved, she said, above all else, the beauty of natural things. A beveled line of hills far across the steppe. The laced ceiling of pine forests. The flowered carpet of river meadows.

But she loved art, too. Often she spent her afternoon alone in the Louvre. She never tired of the statues. Was not the Winged Victory a continual delight? Some day they must go together. She felt he too loved art.

Mercado was puzzled. In an American he would have been offended by the capital A. But in a Russian? Somehow it did not seem *précieuse*. Of course it was probably a stratagem to counteract the impression he had received from meeting her in a cabaret. Even so, was she to be condemned for that? She seemed sincere. Delight is hard to counterfeit, and delight animated her youthful eyes, flushing her cheek.

"Let us stop," she said, "before this statue. It is quite perfect in its frame of trees and shrubs."

In Mercado's eyes the figure was decidedly bad. A sweetish girl feeding the most obvious of doves. Cléopâtre pressed his arm as they paused, urging him to share her gentle sentiment. It would have been cruel to refuse. He professed admiration. Why not, he reflected. The choice was between hypocrisy and callousness. The former was the lesser evil.

"I am happy, John." He had told her to call him John and loved the way her resonant voice sounded the long vowel, "to be with you here. I need so much a *camarade*."

"Are you lonesome?" he inquired.

"You ask that! I, an exile . . . and there is something else."

"Tell me about it," he suggested, not knowing what else to reply.

"No," she said. "Perhaps some day. Shall we go on?"

Mercado found that his appreciation of the garden had been renewed by the years that had passed. Scenes that once had thrilled him and had long since been forgotten now possessed an added poignancy. They moved him by more than their loveliness. He looked down the formal vistas, stirred by an evasive sense of recognition, as if his physical self had been miraculously transported to the valley of his dreams. They strolled between flowers, saying little, unconscious of the world outside the iron fence.

That vague quality, like an unnoticed perfume, which had drawn him to Cléopâtre in the beginning, and had been conspicuously absent earlier in the afternoon, came back revivified. Her nearness satisfied a desire that lay below the threshold of consciousness.

The park was emptying. A few pedestrians passed hurriedly, with a definite goal. The nursegirls and children had disappeared.

"Where shall we eat?" he asked, suddenly aware that he was unusually hungry.

"I will take you to a real Russian restaurant where there is music."

Neither the appearance of the other diners nor the sporadic songs made an impression on Mercado. Nor did he bother with the incomprehensible bill of fare. Cléopâtre willingly took the matter in hand. He found himself looking at her eyes, in anticipation of the pleasant shocks which he received whenever her glance met his. She did not consciously use her eyes as do coquettish women. They were lowered most of the time, and were turned backward when the music was playing.

She was spreading shining black caviar on brown bread, over which she squeezed a few drops of lemon juice. Meanwhile she spoke of her old life in Russia. Her father had been a general. They had lived on a great estate near Kiev. As a little girl she had ridden on hunting expeditions and had learned the use of firearms. Once they had caught a bear cub and raised it in the house. It had been so *drôle* with its clumsy movements and cunning expression. It had been killed in a fight with the dogs. A terrible tragedy. She had a governness in those days, who had taught her French and English, but it was so long ago. She had forgotten all her English.

Anyway the governess hadn't mattered. She and her brother must have been pretty wild. He was always getting into trouble. Once he had broken his arm trying to follow her down a hill. Another time his toboggan had run into a tree and he had nearly died of internal injuries. And then, the peasants! But of course they didn't matter in old Russia. Yes, he was younger than she, two years younger, and had been very delicate as a child. That was what had made him so difficult to handle, so suspicious of every one but herself. They had meant so much to each other until she had mar-

ried. Of course marriage changes everything.
Russian women are not like the others, not like
the French who seek always a lover, or the
Americans who, she had been told, are content
if well provided for. Her husband had been
not only friend and lover but he represented
God. She revered him even to this day.

"We are like that," she said, "we Russians,
when we love.

"But you must teach me English, it will come
back and some day I want to visit your country."

"It is big, like Russia," Mercado said.

"So I have been told," she murmured, "and
there are bandits and cowboys in the mountains."

"Yes," he answered, "but the mountains are
far away."

"I could make a living if I once got there.
I always can, and then we could go to the mountains. You would see. I am never an encum-
brance."

"That I can well believe," Mercado was
pleased because an idiomatic phrase had slipped
so easily from his lips.

"For me," she said, "life is finished. In ten
years I die. Now I must provide for my son

who is on a farm in the country. Later he will take care of himself."

She knew the English word "finished" and repeated it after its French equivalent for emphasis, with the accent on the second syllable. Her lovely voice, when it tentatively essayed an English phrase, added new values to the familiar words.

"Now you're talking nonsense," Mercado replied, his kindly smile negating the harshness of his sentence.

"You don't know me. You Americans. What can you know of the Russian soul? *Nous sommes très originaux.* Let us drink to friendship!"

Mercado felt as if a pledge of tremendous import had been sealed by the click of the glasses. The fluid vibrated in his tumbler. Slowly and solemnly he drank his potion. The mellow wine flowed directly to the pit of his being, warming his heart, elating his spirit.

"Friendship is very beautiful," she continued. "I can never love again."

Mercado reflected that if he were dealing with one of his own countrywomen he would know how to interpret her words. He was convinced that a woman, when she announces she can never love again, is usually conscious of dim stirrings which presage the birth of love. On the other hand, what did he know of Russians?

She continued: "I loved my husband. He was a man! I knew, when he died, my life also was finished. I shall never love again. It is like that with us." Again her expression changed. "Besides," she said, "as a *camarade* I am always the same. When I love I am often *terrible.*"

Her half-closed eyes glittered. The little black points stung like sparks. Mercado found it hard to repress the excitement which surged up at her look. The flash disappeared and was replaced by her usual guileless expression. He was reassured. How could *she* be terrible? Her lips would be soft and tender cushions. He leaned toward them. Something touched his knee. He reached for a hand that eluded his after a passing pressure. He wanted to take her in his arms.

Her startling shifts of mood astonished him. No woman he had ever known had been so stimulating. There was a strangeness about the working of her mind. It seemed so direct, so naïve, and yet he could not follow her train of thought. Each successive sentence was a surprise.

"We Russian women," she added, "are different, you know, very different from the French. If my husband tells me, kill your father and your mother, I kill them. You others are not like that." Then her hand slipped into his, and, as if she were unconscious of it, fondled his, while her eyes sought those distant scenes to which he could not follow. A shiver, partly fascination, partly awe, went rippling down his skin. He was dreaming. He would waken with a start.

Mercado tried to analyze what was happento him. He could not accept, without investigation, even a new sensation. His century demanded the causes of all things. Were Cléopâtre's words rich with mysterious meanings? Were her features as beautiful as they appeared to him? Or was it merely desire, under disguise, that had bewitched his mind, and were these wonders but illusions which would vanish when the desire was gratified? He longed to accept a more romantic interpretation. To believe that Cléopâtre was the complementary soul for whom he had been seeking all his life. The being who possessed the qualities he lacked, who lacked the qualities he possessed, so that together they made a complete personality, perfect and irresistible. Then happiness would be assured, for, in her presence the world would become a place of haunting beauty, and when she was absent, he would dream of her return. Romantic rot!

He pulled himself up short and tried to regard her realistically. A little woman, doubtless possessing a full quota of blemishes. Yet her eyes were filled with music.

"It is necessary," she said, "that I depart. We are not permitted to be late, not even five minutes."

"To the Caveau?" he asked.

"Yes," she said, "are you coming with me?"

"I will take you there."

Then he would leave her and go to bed. He did not wish to dim his memory of the evening by further emotions. There would be plenty of time in the future for gayety and laughter. Now he wanted to be alone, to dream, and to struggle with his dreams.

Thirty-six years of living had taught him to distrust his sanguine temperament. To build, in imagination, lofty palaces was far too easy. The foundations had always been laid in sand and when the edifice crumbled he alone had been the loser. This time he would guard against disillusionment by hoping for nothing. He would accept whatever pleasure the adventure offered and ask for nothing more. Now that he had outgrown the impetuosity of early youth, he should be able to enjoy a love affair and at the same time escape the suffering that had in the past inevitably succeeded the ecstasy. He would cheat fate and prove himself a man.

No more sentimental nonsense. Life has its compensations if one takes them simply. Man's tendency to desert reality for romantic figments is the cause of nearly all his troubles.

He asked for the check. It was surprisingly low. He was convinced that by good luck or intuition he had actually found a woman who demanded little. He felt in top form, and directed the taxi driver to the Caveau as if he were king of the land.

As they sat, close together in the narrow enclosure, he longed to embrace the tenuous figure beside him. He did take her hand. The fingers, strong and silky, reminded him of a cat's paw when the nails are sheathed. He made no further advance. She seemed too remote. It was not yet time.

## CHAPTER FOUR

THE following week passed like a moving picture. Halsey and Mercado had tacitly agreed to postpone the bicycle trip. There was little time for reflection. Engrossed by their new preoccupation, the professors adopted a mode of life which relegated every old interest to an unobtrusive background. Their studies, their American friends, their collegiate habits, underwent a complete though temporary eclipse.

Occasionally the four went out together. More often the couples did not meet until the Caveau reunited them upon its hospitable floor.

There was nothing unusual about Halsey's experience. Vera's animation and high spirits kept him continually on his mettle, while her luxurious body drew a delicious response from his famished sensorium. In her company, he told his friend, he never for a moment was

bored. She was a new type. Her pagan un-
morality and lurid past enthralled the extant
romanticist who had somehow survived the long
years of earnest work. Prematurely staid, he
was rejuvenated by his relapse into a younger
mood.

Halsey learned a great deal about Vera's life.
She had had three husbands. The first had
died shortly after his best friend had killed himself. Rumor had accused Vera of being responsible. She denied complicity, although ad-
mitting she had been the innocent cause. An
artillery officer had relieved her of a second
husband. The third was in Paris, but did not
live with her. Nothing mattered, she often
said, but love, and how can you know if you love
until you have tried it out?

"Very true," Halsey replied, trying not to be
shocked.

During the war Vera had been a Sister of
Mercy. Many a hospital ward had longed for
her daily visit. Now life was less exciting.
Still things happened. And her enigmatic eyes
smiled at Halsey. As for her, she had nothing
to conceal. Her life might be an open book in
which all the world could read, for all she

cared. Halsey's curiosity was only checked by his difficulty with the language.

Meanwhile Vera, who in the beginning had taken the shy, mild stranger as an exotic curio, became increasingly fond of him. For her also it was a new experience. His technique, or rather lack of it, induced her to make the advances. As a result, she soon assumed the masculine rôle and found it pleasant. Especially as she could only get so far with him and no further. The gentle friend, who seemed like clay in her hands, could be led up to a certain point . . . when all at once he became obdurate. Unable to fathom the difficulty, his inhibitions were quite beyond the reach of her imagination, Vera's perversity was aroused. She would bring this American to her feet, she, who had been adored by regiments, was not going to be foiled by a small blond man with a winsome mustache and gentle eyes.

The exertion of her will automatically made the object of its effort desirable. The more Halsey eluded her, the more she wanted him. The chase became furious. And he, tremendously flattered, released from moral scruples by her past, and from temperance by the prohibition law, indulged in a series of dithyrambic orgies which made the good times of his youth anemic by comparison. He felt like a boy who, on meeting a pretty girl, suddenly discovers he has outgrown childish games. Of course, Halsey worked out, in his dry way, a passable philosophical defense for this break with his code.

The orgy, he argued, fills a definite human need. All the ancient races worshiped Dionysus in some form or other. Calvinism, endeavoring to suppress his rites, has been successful only when the pressure of existence has taken the entire energy of man. Thus during American pioneer days many thought Bacchus was dead forever. Now that the struggle is less severe, the old god turns in his grave. Unless he finds some normal egress, the nation will suffer from the maladies that result when a natural desire is suppressed.

Halsey appealed to Vera's maternal instinct. If asked, she would have vehemently denied regretting her sterility. She was childless from conviction. Some women were born mothers, some are born to love. She belonged to the latter category and any obstacle to the free expression of her various passions would be against her true nature.

Such was her conscious and sincere belief. Yet certain gestures, and the little superfluous attentions by which she revealed her affection, would have indicated to a sensitive observer a maternal phase, which not even systematic starvation had succeeded in subverting.

Of quite another character was Cléopâtre's technique, by which is meant the subconscious tactics of her femininity rather than the conduct prescribed by her intellect. Apparently self-contained, rarely effusive or exuberant, she would have appeared indifferent to the attentions of Mercado if it had not been for those odd flashes which seemed to escape by accident. Particularly her eyes would now and then convey, in one intense, absorbing, ecstatic look, both a promise and a denial. They seemed to proffer love, that mysterious transcendent love which hurdles all impediments, while at the same time they refuted the coldness that her restraint implied. However, it was difficult for Mercado to believe her eyes after the instant had passed, for nothing in her habitual demeanor supported such an interpretation. Perhaps he saw a meaning in those looks which was not there, a fiction created by desire.

The only corroborating evidence was an odd comment or two which suggested a willingness to throw her lot in with his. For instance, her wish to go with him to America. Did it mean that she took him seriously, or was it but a casual remark thrown off by hazard, which expressed nothing more than dissatisfaction with her present mode of life? He felt the question was insoluble until he knew her better. Meanwhile this quandary, added to the anomalies inherent in her character, intensified his interest until his intercourse with Cléopâtre monopolized his days. He could think of nothing else. His mornings were spent anticipating the afternoons.

Yet now and again he laughed at himself because of the importance she was assuming in his life. He knew that at the end of the month he would return to his work and never see her again. He knew, or thought he knew, that within a day or two of his departure she would be forgotten. Nevertheless, he continually caught himself, while writing a letter or riding a bus, reconstructing some moment of the night before. It might be a glance from her eyes, evanescent as the light of a firefly, for she did not look at him often and when she did her whole expression changed. Or it might be a sentence, usually one of her rare English phrases, which he would discover himself repeating. One afternoon they went to the movies at her suggestion. She had wanted to see a picture of prerevolutionary Russia. The show, to Mercado's surprise, was American. However, the plot was laid in Moscow and the Hollywood experts had reconstructed various corners of the Kremlin from photographs. It made Cléopâtre very happy. She did not seem to notice the bedraggled eucalyptus trees which could not have been familiar features of her native country. It was not a bad picture, and if she was pleased he could not object.

One scene showed an avenue barred off by a fence on which was posted: "Street closed for repairs." The next day, while riding in a taxi they were halted by the usual: *"Rue barrée."* Cléopâtre, looking straight ahead, with a quizzical smile around the corners of her mouth, said: "Street clos-en," quite accurately except for the delightful Russian "r" and the incorrect termination. That was all. And yet this phrase, in which there was no particular beauty or aptness, kept recurring to him at the most inopportune moments.

Mercado sometimes wondered if he could be falling in love. He did not think so, chiefly because he had no overwhelming desire to possess her. She attracted him tremendously, but he felt no press or hurry. He had never enjoyed a vacation so much, and was quite content to let things take their natural course. He did not become suspicious of this reasoning till afterwards. At that time he assumed that the exigency of passion measures the temperature of love.

Her image had become extraordinarily real to him. He visualized, on waking in the morning, her brazen hair falling, like the curved sides of an upturned boat, from the parting on her head to the jade grapes that swung beneath her ears. He could not fix the dark eyes that looked out from this martial frame, for they were never, even in his mind's eyes, the same for two successive instants. Sometimes they were the eyes of a northern goddess, out of the Scandinavian sagas, dynamic and cold. Sometimes they were the eyes of a nomadic queen who, veiled and recumbent, could only be approached through the triangular flap of a tent. A mysterious queen dreamed of in adolescence.

Even her body had become lovely to him. On their first meeting it had seemed too full— his canons of taste had still been American. But no longer. Now he could appreciate her breasts, firm and high, and her wide sinuous hips. The diffidence of her eyes was denied by her upright carriage. She walked, toes pointing straight in front, as he imagined an Iroquois squaw had walked, ready to carry a load on her back and to move evenly ahead for days on end beneath a ceiling of interlaced hemlocks.

With such a companion it was a rare pleasure to explore the attractions of the city. Several times they joined the populace and rode the galloping pigs at the street fair. The more violent the motion the more Cléopâtre liked it. Under the influence of the pervasive music which was the product of several melodies and incongruous instruments mingling in one bizarre, modernistic effect, even Mercado lost his self-consciousness. He realized the absurdity of his position, he would not like to have been seen by one of his pupils, astride a ponderous porker, beside a rollicking female with hair unfurled, but he consoled himself by the thought that even if he had been seen, the spectator would not have credited the evidence of his eyes. And then there were sideshows with women wrestlers and obstetrical wax works; a flea circus whose stalwart trainer bared a spotted arm that served as his pets' banquet board. Cléopâtre loved the animals too, though Mercado was disturbed by their mangy condition and their harassed expression. As for the shooting galleries, he could hardly tear her away from them and had repeatedly to suffer the humiliation of defeat. Cléopâtre, however, assured him optimistically that he would become a first-rate shot with a little practice.

More often they visited the haunts of the Russians and consumed quantities of tomatoes, cucumbers and eggplant, the latter curiously prepared. Eggplant, she explained, served among the poorer Russians for caviar. Afterwards there was always *borsch*, into which a round ball of chopped meat was dropped, and after that . . . but Mercado could seldom eat his way further. He enjoyed the preliminaries too much.

One day the four of them took the little river boat to Saint-Cloud and wandered through the village while the sun was setting over the hill. This expedition was not very successful, for the boat was overcrowded and the heat excessive in such close quarters. Mercado even escorted Cléopâtre to a Russian students' ball which astonished him because the young people were so like those he was familiar with at home. He expected the exotic quality, which he found at the Caveau and in Cléopâtre, to inhere in all Russians.

Of the many beliefs, so oddly assorted in Cléopâtre's mind, one in particular puzzled Mercado. The Platonic ideal, which she professed, did not accord, he thought, with her character or her training. Yet she repeatedly asserted, with apparent sincerity, that she did not want to sleep with him. She wanted a *camarade*. Passion, she claimed, made a relationship ephemeral.

Mercado considered this a superstition. It was based on the conception of man as a hunter. Possibly it was true for some, but it hardly applied to the average teacher of literature, at least in America.

However, it was difficult to argue out abstractions in a language foreign to them both. Time would solve the question.

Occasionally, when he recalled what he had heard of the physical freedom of Russian women, he felt her standoffishness was a ruse, subconscious perhaps, but meant to increase his infatuation. Yet it seemed hardly credible that she was capable of even this subtlety if the naïveté of her conversation be taken into account. And there were conscious lapses from this Platonic ideal. Her offer, under a flush of emotion, when the imminency of his departure happened suddenly to rise before them, that he go with her to Dinard and lie on the yellow sand in sound of the wash of the waves, was disquieting, or encouraging, depending on the point of view.

Mercado answered that it was impossible because of the inflexible nature of his engagement, but promised to come back to her soon. She naturally did not believe him, for he had spoken of the projected bicycle trip, and would not consent, at that moment, to spend a week-end in the country with him, for which there was ample time.

On their sixth evening together they drank and dined at the Caveau, then went over to Konyaks for breakfast. Their friendship had not appreciably advanced. Mercado felt little more intimate than he had during their first walk in the gardens of the Luxembourg one week before. Halsey, tired out, had left somewhat earlier and they were left alone except for the other guests. Cléopâtre knew many of these, a fact which fluttered Mercado and made him vaguely angry.

The spontaneous character of the entertainment, the hum of language completely foreign and the shape of the room, windowless, tapestried, made him feel that several centuries had been left outside the door. In addition, the glow, which, like a magic potion always inspired him when he was close to Cléopâtre, brought more than a sense of well-being. It transformed the world. Looking up he noticed that her features, which had been merely pretty, were become resplendent. A radiance, gentle and dazzlingly beautiful, shone from her eyes. An enchantment, that required all the restraint of his upbringing to resist, curled the edge of her lips. Suddenly a veil, like a shower of music, was drawn between them and the other guests.

He took her hand. The veil, besides its other properties, destroyed self-consciousness. He felt as if they were isolated. As if the *mise en scène* were solely for their benefit. He watched the rise and fall of her breasts as he held himself back in order to draw the uttermost drop of the exquisite moment before their lips touched. Her long lashes flickered like the wings of a humming bird. He kissed her. It was the first time. He did not think until later how strange it was to kiss her for the first time before people she knew.

The veil became translucent. Then the music and color slowly approached as light comes in when one wakens from sleep.

"You are adorable," he murmured. "I love you."

"John," she said, "you mustn't say that."

"And why not, dear?"

"It makes me afraid." She shivered as one does in a wood when a slight movement makes one aware of the mysteries that are hidden in the shadows. She smiled at him. She had not been displeased.

"If one could hold it!" Mercado exclaimed, continuing to clutch her fingers as if thereby the intangible emotion could be retained. "It is inconceivable to me that given the elements, which are nothing more nor less than you and I, we cannot always have the ecstasy. The response seems as inevitable as a chemical reaction."

"One who has loved," she said, as if he had not spoken, "never dares love again. It is too terrible."

"But what else is there?" Mercado asked, dropping the train of his thought to try and meet hers.

"Adventure, excitement, friendship. Things one can keep outside."

"But how can you value them? You who have known love? Are they not insignificant in comparison?" Mercado did not feel himself on sure ground. His one great love affair had brought him little joy and long years of regret. As for the little ones . . . In retrospect they seemed little indeed.

"I have a secret," she said, "I must tell you."

"No secret," he said, "can have the least importance."

"My brother," her expression had become very grave, "killed my husband."

"The past does not exist for . . ." Then the meaning of her words penetrating . . . "but what was that you said?"

She did not answer. A tear formed in the corner of each eye.

"My dear, what do you mean?" he asked.

She raised her lashes and laughed softly.

"Let us drink," she said and lifted the glass to the level of her lips.

"Something about your brother," he reminded her.

"I do not remember," she replied. "To friendship!"

Mercado leaned back, relaxing. A crisis had been passed.

"Take me," she burst out suddenly, "to America, to Mexico. There are bandits in Mexico. That is life. Then one forgets."

"It sounds good to me," Mercado replied, "but it needs money." The late professor of literature gayly rigged out in chaps, sombrero, revolver and lasso!

"I can earn money," she said, "anywheres. Especially in New York."

"And your brother would come along?"

"You are not funny, John. You pretend not to understand."

"Not at all. I should think he would make a fine bandit."

"John," she said, "let us go for a drive in the Bois."

Mercado, though still under the spell, tried to do some serious thinking during the long ride down the avenue. He was particularly struck by the matter-of-fact way he had considered Cléopâtre's absurd proposal. Her voice and personality had made it seem reasonable. And if all the world were searched for an outrageous idea surely nothing could be found to surpass her proposition. Neither of them spoke Spanish. It wasn't worth discussing. Yet not only had it not seemed ridiculous at the time, but quite feasible. An escape from a life he loathed. A definite break with the bonds that held him. Consequently he must conclude that Cléopâtre was able to make him lose his wits. Something to be watched out for, Mercado decided, or he'd run into trouble.

He was pleased, at heart, that their relationship had moved on to a more intimate level. His vanity had been hurt by the apparent inefficaciousness of his attentions. He had begun to fear he had lost his charm. Especially as Halsey had been getting on so famously. Her offer restored his confidence.

## CHAPTER FIVE

AS he waited for Cléopâtre the following evening at the Café de Versailles, Mercado reflected upon the nature of time. Seven days had passed since he had walked in the garden with Cléopâtre. Seven days during which they had talked, eaten, danced and played together. And she had been more elusive on the sixth day than on the first. Then something happened. He had looked for an instant beneath her mask. Their lips had touched. Never again would be feel the same toward her. One instant had accomplished more than a week of companionship. Evidently time was of little importance outside the sphere of material things and it was stupid of him to fret because Cléopâtre, as usual, was fifteen minutes late.

He noticed the two young men who were drinking at the next table. They spoke English, but their emery chins, blue shirts and eager ties indicated that they had joined the confraternity of international artists, abandoning their national ideals. One of them was telling a long anecdote. "It's all perfectly preposterous. The street I live on—what *is* the name of it, you know, just around the corner from the Gare Montparnasse—well, anyhow, it has two hotels that look exactly alike. Don't know how I failed to notice it. Last Monday night I was coming home, stinko, well, you know, as usual . . ."

A covey of buses rumbled by, muffling his words. Mercado looked at him curiously; a poet, one would say, by his hollow cheeks and inlaid eyes. Then his mind leaped across the city. Halsey was taking Vera to the Champs-Elysées theater. Funny old Halsey! It would probably do him good if he didn't become too serious. And Vera could be trusted on that score, she was no fool. Neither was she as attractive as Halsey supposed. Now, for his own taste, she was too obvious. Nothing to lead one on. Cléopâtre was just the opposite. . . .

The voice at the next table boomed out: "I couldn't get in, and I said to myself, 'Sam, old man, there's some one in your room.' And so, obviously, I looked through *my* keyhole into *my* room, and there I saw an old man taking off about six yards of French shirt. So I pounded on my door, but the white-haired bugger paid no attention. Then I started kicking at the panels, I mean, well, the natural thing to do, and the concierge came up, and I threatened to call the police. No action. So then, of course, I got hold of an *agent* with a beastly long mustache, but the concierge convinced him I was crazy. Really. There was nothing left to do but go walking round and round the block.

"Suddenly, there was my hotel. I shouted for the *cordon* and climbed the stairs, but my door was locked. I looked through the keyhole, and there sat the same old gudgeon, in his night-shirt, reading Paris *Galant*. It was too much, really. An obscene newspaper. I became quite angry and began to break down the door.

"It was all so logical, I mean not logical at all, but it seemed that way. And there, in a moment, stood the same concierge. I was very firm. I told him I needed sleep. He left, and this time he was going to fetch the police. I really couldn't bother myself, I was very tired, so I walked downstairs, and the concierge's door stood open. That's the whole story. I stumbled in and went to bed with his wife. Really. She took it very nicely, for when the *agents* came . . ."

"Have you been waiting long? I am so sorry."

Mercado rose. Cléopâtre seated herself beside him and started to explain that some one had come to see her just as she was starting off.

Mercado paid no attention. He was trying to catch the end of the story, but the speaker had lowered his voice.

"John, you are *distrait*. Are you angry with me?"

"My dear," he said, "how could that be?"

She evoked the softness which lies close to the surface in Mercado. He took her hand. The unfinished anecdote was forgotten.

Yet something was wrong with the evening. Mercado concluded, when they had settled down in their favorite Russian restaurant, that they were suffering the inevitable reaction. They had reached, the night before, an emotional height which could not be maintained. Consequently their normal intercourse seemed, in its afterglow, relatively insipid. He doubted if

Cléopâtre shared his feeling. Her sensitiveness was of another kind. Perhaps a drink would help. They had been so temperate. She always said she did not like to drink. He wondered if she meant it. Halsey had had a very different experience with Vera. But Halsey was more of a drinker anyway. Still it would be interesting to test her sincerity. . . .

"What have you ordered to drink?" he asked.

"White wine," she said; "it isn't bad."

"I'm tired of it. *Vin ordinaire!* I'd just as soon drink water."

"Shall I ask for the list? They don't carry much of a selection here."

"Let us have vodka."

His own request startled him. He had never tasted vodka. It had the glamor of forbidden things, suggesting drunken peasants rolling on stoves, Mitya Karamazov summoning a whole town to his party, coachmen whipping four horses into a gallop. But now that he had suggested it he would not back down. He insisted.

"We *will* have vodka. I shall like it. You can drink for once."

A small carafe, the size which holds *un quart*

*de vin,* filled with a colorless liquid, indistinguishable from water, and two liqueur glasses, straightway appeared.

"Wait!" she said. "I must prepare the caviar."

Her fingers were deftly spreading the little black eggs over the rough brown bread.

"First a bite, then the vodka in one swallow. That is how we drink in Russia."

Though shy about sampling the new beverage so drastically, Mercado could not gracefully back down at this stage. He swallowed it. So did Cléopâtre. Then he filled the glasses, confident of his ability to drink with any woman, even though she be Russian. The approximate ratio, according to Cléopâtre, was two bites to one swallow. The carafe had shortly to be refilled.

"I like the taste," he said, "I foresee vodka will be my favorite drink. It is too bad I've wasted all these years unaware of its preëminence."

"Let us drink," she said, "to Russia!"

"To Russia!" he echoed not averse, though the Russia to which he drank was not, he felt, the Russia which she toasted.

"Russia exists no longer. All has gone down in the ruin. Yet it will rise again. It will rise from the ashes. My Russia! . . . John, you would have loved it. There is something of the Russian in you. You are not like the others."

"Nothing lasts," his voice was saying; "all things come to an end and new things take their places." His words were familiar to him. He had said them before. They were the crux of his philosophy. Yet he felt as if some one else were speaking through him. His real self had somehow became detached from the self that was sitting there. "Life is change, we only bruise ourselves by willing permanence." His speaking self was talking foolishness. She was paying no attention. The moment was fraught with things more important than old ideas. And yet one had to pretend to talk and to listen so that the action could go on undisturbed, as if unnoticed.

"I love Americans. They are like us, original. We will go to places together. I will show you. *Les Apaches*. They are not like the other French. *Une boîte très originale!*"

"Won't you go to the Caveau this evening?"

"You ask? The Caveau is not for my

friends. It is too expensive. I must, for my child, work there. But I shall take dancing lessons. I know the peasant dances, and give exhibitions. It will be much better."

Mercado, whom one might describe as an introspective drinker, began to wonder whether the effect of vodka differed from that of other alcoholic stimulants. It seemed to intensify his perceptions and emotions without befuddling his reasoning faculties. Its potency, on the other hand, had been much exaggerated. He felt fine. It was a grand party. Cléopâtre was adorable.

Mercado possessed, to a remarkable degree, that peculiar quality which enables one to watch, as a spectator, the scenes which one's kinetic self enacts. The effect of drink or of emotional stress was to increase the detachment between his two personalities so that the spectator eventually became impotent and could not interfere in any way with the performance of the actor. After their second carafe, Mercado could only regard his words and actions with the interest and amazement of an outsider. The spectator struggled ineffectually against the romanticism of his other self.

When Cléopâtre, after they had finished their soup, shoved her plate away and exclaimed: "Let us go!" Mercado called for the check and set forth, without a qualm, upon a night of adventure.

He was in high spirits. With the liveliest anticipation, he listened to Cléopâtre directing the taxi driver to some difficult address near the Boule Miche.

The night air seemed to have a sobering effect, though the light clusters wavered uncertainly, as the taxi swung around corners, in and out of the narrow streets. Mercado mused over the dogmatic advice which had slipped, so casually, from his brain. Why should he of all people preach: "Life is change, one can only bruise oneself by willing permanence"? For him, life had not been change. It had been permanence and monotony. How he hated it! And yet it had taken him fifteen years to make a break and even it was only provisional. The philosophy he had professed was the philosophy he would have liked to practice but which he had, in life, timorously rejected. Was that true of most men? Did they preach what they failed to practice? Or was it merely that he lacked strength of character?

As for Cléopâtre, did she practice what she preached? Or was she another woman masquerading in a romantic guise which was the opposite of her real self? Her face belied her words. Her eyes belied her face. He was getting nowhere. "I love Americans. They are like us, original." She knew little, and yet, in a sense, her statement was true. How cynically a Frenchman would have taken her. She felt the difference in his attitude. But a more accurate adjective would be romantic. A quality Balzac had exhausted for the French.

"John," she said, leaning against him, "you are not displeased?"

"Of course not," he replied. "On the contrary. Your nearness brings to the ride a beauty . . ."

"I like you, John. You will be a good *camarade* to me."

"Cléopâtre!" He kissed her. On impulse. If he had thought he would have hesitated. The feel of her strong body as it alternately relaxed and became taut, gave him a sense of elemental force which quickened the beat of his heart and pushed the uncertain musings of his mind far back.

He released her when the quandary of the driver reminded him of their destination. They were seeking an address. He regretted the shortness of their journey. The chauffeur was insistent, finally, with an air of triumph, pointing out the number.

Down they stumbled, along dark, low passages. Lamps, black smoke twisting above their yellow flames, indicated tortuous steps. A lumpy man flattened himself against the masonry to let them pass with a *"Bonsoir, Monsieurdame."* His voice grated like rusty hinges.

They were stopped by a door, studded with hand-cut spikes. Faintly from behind hummed blended voices and music. She seized the great iron ring and let it fall. The clash reverberated ominously. The door swung in. They lurched toward smoke-fringed faces.

Crash! The floor had given under them. A hundred mouths split to blow metallic laughs. They were clinging to each other. The floor had dropped only some inches. They were on a trap door. "The pit, Madame, where guests used to be received."

At the end of the low ceiling an angular figure had paused in his song. He waved invit-
ingly over the intermediate heads. Cléopâtre
started picking a way toward him, followed by
Mercado. The figure turned its profile, dropping, like a monkey wrench, a hard square jaw.
They were sitting down. A table and two stools
had miraculously appeared.

"*Du vin blanc,*" Mercado said to the red-
shirted, white-aproned ruffian that leaned over
them.

A bass voice issued from the monkey wrench,
rasping rhythmically to the moaning of a hidden accordeon. All the faces turned toward
the singer. Mercado sighed with relief.

He tried to make out the words. Only a few
did he recognize. It must be argot, he decided.

Two huge men, so close he smelled them, sat
at the next table. In the unshaven bulbous face
of the nearest, were set two china marbles
which pointed, Mercado felt, at him, without
seeing him. Mercado could not keep himself
from looking at them. They drew his eyes as
a serpent's draw a monkey's.

"Drinken!" Cléopâtre was saying. "Trin-
ken!" Her languages had evidently become

mixed. Mercado explained that he had already ordered wine.

"Everybody must drink to Russia," she shouted as the beats of the handclapping . . . one, two . . . one, two, three . . . which had followed the song, died down. A liter of white wine was approaching their table by a devious route.

"More glasses!" No one paid attention to the latter request, which was hardly necessary for tumblers appeared on all sides.

Cléopâtre filled the nearest ten or so, to the brim. "More wine, John." She noticed him for the first time since arriving. "We must drink, all, all . . ." She rose to her feet. "To Russia!"

Mercado was feeling uncomfortable. He was oppressed, in the first place, by the proximity of so many hideous faces. Though he had been more crowded in New York subway crushes, never had human countenances seemed so little human. It was not their foreignness, that he would have relished, but their animality. He was among a new species. Besides, the two specimens nearest him were far too big. He was not a little man, but he felt minute and delicate beside their beefsteak lips and matted arms and chests. The china marbles were particularly demoralizing. If only they would respond to his glance. If only they had some expression, even ferocity. But stoniness . . .

He felt a horror akin to that he had known as a child, when, for the first time, he had slept alone. The room had been big and, in the far corner, a towel rack had projected over the washstand. An invisible gas jet had thrown the suspended linens into relief while their grotesque shadows had flickered on the wall behind. These had assumed horrible shapes, sometimes bestial, sometimes demoniac. His hair had stood up on his head, which he would bury beneath the bed-clothes. And still, the terror, stalking in the far corner.

Mercado's reflective self, realizing the absurdity of a mature man succumbing to such a childish mood, tried in vain to throw it off. No reasoning seemed of avail. He told himself the cellar was merely a dive frequented by such workmen as he passed every day. It did no good. A supernatural horror continued to invest his surroundings.

"Nice gen-tel-men!" Cléopâtre remarked in her ornate labored English. Then, leaning across Mercado, she addressed Marble Eyes: "Drink, you must drink with me."

The monster raised his glass phlegmatically.

"No. Touch glasses. All of you." She insisted as Mercado hung back. Grimly he clicked his tumbler against his neighbor's. The old Alma Mater, he thought, has certain advantages.

"Real Apaches," she whispered in his ear. "Splen-deed."

The second giant, whom he named Cyclops for his closed left eye, nudged his friend's knee like a schoolgirl. Mercado shivered.

"I want them to take us to a real *boîte du nuit*." Cléopâtre continued. "Change places with me."

He complied reluctantly. He had never hated any one so thoroughly as the two strangers. But he did not have time to think how he could refuse her request. The habit of acceding to a woman's wishes is so deeply rooted as to be nearly automatic. When he had shifted his position he cursed himself for not having frankly refused. There was no point in post-

poning the crisis. A new liter of wine had arrived.

"Drinken, John, drinken!"

Mercado wondered why she had dropped into
pidgin English when she addressed him. He
became very sullen.

Cléopâtre was effusively making up to her
new friends. Mercado listened in. She spoke
fast and low. He caught the word "Cowboy,"
pronounced Kooboy. She seemed to be using it
in a derisive sense. "We can get rid of the
Kooboy." A flush crept up to his ears. He was
furious and could do nothing.

"You take me to a new place. I want to meet
*les vrais Apaches*," she said over and over
again. Mercado squirmed as the Kooboy,
sounding incredibly ugly, knocked his ears once
more. In telling about it he laughed over the
aversion this innocent designation had inspired
in him. He explained that the contempt she
conveyed by her tone had quite eradicated even
his sense of humor. He had had enough to
drink to make him react single-mindedly. He
only felt that a foul creature, who had lifted
him to the skies by her kisses, was now degrading
him. If he would have had half a chance, he

believed he would have smashed the carafe on Marble Eyes' head. But against such a multitude!

However, he refused to buy more wine. The songs continued. The smoke, like stratified rock, hung over the floor of heads. Cléopâtre kept on talking to the men beside her. Mercado paid no further attention. A girl at another table tried to make up to him. He smiled instinctively but had become too dull really to notice.

"John, take me away."

She had to speak twice before he heard. Insensibly he paid the bill and led her toward the door. The crowd had thinned. He became somewhat apprehensive for his safety but not acutely, for he did not even look behind him.

The street was a dim sounding-board on which their footsteps played a syncopated melody. The boulevard, for all he knew, might lie in either direction. He chose the left, for a glimmer of light promised more familiar surroundings. Cléopâtre took his arm. Mercado's only reaction was to wonder if, in case of need, he could free it readily. He felt they were being followed, but was too numb to be other than indifferent. His only precautionary measure was to listen closely for the sound of approaching steps. He visualized the chalky boots of Marble Eyes falling and rising behind him.

At the first cross street a taxi swung in front of them. His raised hand halted it. He helped in Cléopâtre, following immediately after. Two heads were even with the open window. She was bidding Cyclops good night. "To-morrow then you will take me where I shall see *les vrais apaches?*"

A vague assent was murmured.

Cléopâtre set the hour and the place. Formal handshakes were exchanged.

"And what is your address?" Mercado asked.

She told him. He relayed it to the driver. The gears ground.

Mercado's behavior during the drive, unless one bears in mind his peculiar make-up, is difficult to understand. When they started off he was outwardly dull and phlegmatic, inwardly furious and hurt. When they arrived he was holding Cléopâtre in his arms. Such a dénouement was possible because his reflective self had withdrawn to a great distance. For it was his reflective self that attempted to follow a consistent line of conduct, that remembered grudges, and judged impulses by their relation to the future and the past. Mercado's reflective self was still functioning, but from the middle of the orchestra. It had become simply a spectator and could not interfere with the performance by even a shouted suggestion. It could applaud, groan, shudder, suffer and laugh, but his active self was no more influenced by its emotions than a tragedian is affected by the enthusiasm or apathy of his audience.

At the same time his active self was tired from a surfeit of emotions. For the time being it ceased to react independently and accepted any outside stimulus with equal willingness. Thus their motion through the darkness, across the Seine, under the arches of the Louvre, along the wide Avenue de l'Opera, routed his anger and disgust, while Cléopâtre's physical magnetism, which lapsed when others were with them, revived as soon as they were seated side by side on the narrow seat.

Consequently she slipped into his arms to his astonishment, for he did not know how she got there, and to his shame, for he felt that so rapid a reconciliation was undignified.

Especially undignified since she refrained from anything in the nature of an apology, even from the expression of regret. What had been, she seemed to feel, had to be and therefore was right. Mercado had a furtive admiration for her attitude, so unlike his own, even though it was hardly flattering. Such composure must, he thought, be a wonderful help in the tribulations of life.

The taxi drew up before a hotel in the quarter behind the Madeleine. The moment had come to say good night and good-by. Mercado had accepted as a matter of course that the good-by would be final. The next day would see him on the road. His wearied mind was incapable of further imaginings.

"John," she said, "I do not want to go to bed."

"And what do you want?" he asked, gently enough, reflecting that another man would probably have replied in a more forceful manner.

"I feel queer. Not too well. It is necessary that I dance. I want to dance with you. I like the way you dance."

"You wish, I infer, to be taken to the Caveau."

He decided as she spoke to take her there and then, casually, to disappear.

Mercado, incapable of a brutal gesture, evades, if it be possible, a direct rebuff no matter how imperative the need. Aware of this quality he is undecided whether to blame it on weakness or on kindliness.

"No," she said, "you are *drôle*. I would be well received. I want to dance with *you*. In no time at all I will be all right.

"John, take me to Le Paradis."

He stared at her, astonished at such preposterous impudence.

"I understand French, you know," he said, meaning to remind her of her Kooboy speech. He was not sure if she realized that he had understood it. Although they habitually conversed in the French tongue she had seemed, while at the dive, to believe she had to address him in English.

But Cléopâtre passed off his remark as if it

had been unsaid. She was directing the driver to a street in Montmartre.

"But I haven't given my assent," Mercado weakly interrupted.

"You will like Le Paradis," she said. "It is a popular dance hall full of *types très originaux*."

"John," lifting his hand to her lips, turning it over and pressing softly against the palm, "you will be a good *camarade* when you understand me better. We Russians, we are different from you others."

To make the best of a bad situation, Mercado accepted it. He felt like a dreamer in an endless dream. The night stretched infinitely ahead. Its end was inconceivable. He was doomed, for ever and ever, to conduct a willful erratic spirit through diverse scenes each with an appropriate and contrary emotion. Once he gave up all pretense at control, the sensation was not unpleasant. They were gliding under a young moon to Le Paradis, whatever that might be, and he was kissing the strongest, softest, most exciting lips . . .

Twisted strings of lights, red and white, invited them to enter a foyer of polished mirrors.

Though it nowise resembled the places from which they had come, he felt as if he had been there before. Evidently he was destined to enter many foyers. He wondered if the vodka had anything to do with his phantasmic sensations.

A great crowd surged toward them, garish, cheap and overdressed. Lurid colors and dyed hair. Dress suits on which the tails hung awry. Street suits in florid checks and stripes. Wing collars compressing redundant Adam's apples. Floating ribbons and painted lips.

*"Voici, Monsieur!"*

They were being led through the hurly-burly. Mercado complied, amenable to any outside direction. Le Paradis compressed, in one great ballroom, two dancing floors and two orchestras. The comparatively empty section, to which they were conducted, was reserved for champagne drinkers. He did not even demur at this, but chose, at random, a vintage, *goût Americain.*

"Excuse me, please!" Cléopâtre left him alone for an indeterminable time. The music beat upon his brain. He sipped the wine. Episodes from his past flickered through his

[ 124 ]

head. Love episodes that he treasured, although in each an element of unfulfillment evoked the depressing sentiment of regret. Never more, he dramatically resolved, would he hold back. Better to suffer the pangs of remorse than the anguish of regret. He would take, come what may, what he could.

As for Cléopâtre, she was playing with him. Which had no terror so long as he was playing with her. Two disappointed, sophisticated, pathetic, human beings, going through a comedy so that at moments they might forget the misery of being alive. Rather nice that. An esthetic ideal. Drama should not be confined to the theater. Why not romp a bit in actual life so long as it was fair and both were acting? He could do his part, no doubt without distinction, but adequately. As for her, she made every girl he'd ever known . . .

A white face, dimly serious, seemed to say: "One must not play with love. It is the sin against the Holy Ghost."

Mercado, to turn his thought, gulped down the contents of his glass, pulled out his watch, scrutinized the dial without noting the time, and tried to concentrate on his surroundings.

A fair percentage of the revelers were American. One could tell the men by the way they carried their heads. Strange, he reflected, that a new race had already formed, different from those that preceded it, and as definite as the races of ancient lineage. Of course, traces of their inheritances still persisted, but superimposed were new and striking characteristics which were doubly conspicuous here, where so many nations mingled. He compared an American negro to a Senegalese. The former had a swing to his shoulder and a forwardness in his eye that the latter utterly lacked. And yet, the negro was least American of all the melting-pot's ingredients. Though not least if the effect of him on America be under consideration rather than the effect of America on him. It would be well, he felt, if the negro could give a little more to his kidnapers in the way of spontaneity and joy of life.

His paler compatriots seemed peculiarly destitute of these gifts. Mercado searched out from the multitude, faces that were sober and strained, faces that were painfully trying to enjoy themselves, faces that were bored. In most cases they belonged to his countrymen.

Perhaps it is owing to their habit of trying to give their wives a good time. But he had to discard this hypothesis, for the majority were with French cocottes whose escorts had the same bored look when they weren't obviously tight.

"I suppose," he concluded, "they don't talk French, the class that come here, and of course there is not much fun in it then."

He had gradually attained a more equable humor though still far from the flamboyant exhilaration which had whirled him about earlier in the evening.

Just as he was beginning to grow impatient, Cléopâtre returned, looking a little pale but as full of life as before.

"Let us dance," she said, after draining her glass.

They danced. Awkwardly in the beginning but not so awkwardly as on their first meeting. After a while they stopped to drink their wine; then retook the floor. It was nearly empty. But three other couples contested its smooth expanse. Cléopâtre began to catch his rhythm or rather his interpretation of the music's rhythm. Enjoying the feel of her sturdy body, so close to his, Mercado gave himself up more freely to

[ 127 ]

the motion, embroidering the simple beat with fanciful interpolations.

The music gradually became a ruling force. Its sway was absolute. No outside stimuli affected the closed web of their interwoven sensations.

Dancing they became one body, an integrated entity. The rhythm was passed, as in a relay race, from jazz band to string orchestra and back again without a stop. First one couple, then another, left the floor. Mercado and Cléopâtre continued unperturbed. They were still dancing when the others returned after a rest; still dancing when, a second time, they were deserted on the waxed square.

Of a sudden Mercado noticed his arm was limp, his feet ached, his back had a kink near the middle, his face was streaming. He reflected that no matter how rapturous a dance may be, a time comes when the flesh refuses. It is usual, he knew, for the man to tire sooner than his partner, for the man directs the motion and supports a fraction of the woman's weight. Still he rebelled at the thought that Cléopâtre could outlast him. He said nothing and kept on dancing. The pleasure was gone. His pains increased. His joints seemed devoid of lubricants . . .

The situation became desperate. He would not give in, and yet, if he did not, his legs might collapse from under him. Already his poor left arm had crumpled and his right felt paralyzed. An idea came to him.

"I cannot dance," he said, "the tango."

"But this is not a tango," she observed. "It's a fox-trot."

"No," Mercado replied, "it's the Fuegean tango," and stopped dead.

"It was marvelous," she murmured; "you dance superbly."

"Never learned it," he mumbled as he led her back to the table.

When two glasses of champagne had restored his vitality he said: "But you are strong! I would never have suspected you were capable of such endurance."

"It was nothing," she answered deprecatingly.

"I don't agree with you," Mercado argued. "Physical strength in a woman indicates a lively wit." He was talking nonsense. He felt like talking nonsense.

"John," she seemed very pleased with his remark, "you are eccentric. Americans are like Russians."

"Appearances," he said, "are captious."

"I wish," she answered, "you could ride horseback with me. That is life. Only two weeks I've been at the Caveau. Before I worked in a factory. It did not bring enough money. One must eat. But I cannot do as the others. I am not like that, John."

"You prefer the Apaches."

"I like wild things. My father is a warrior. Force is real. Tame people are *ennuyeux*."

"Well, you shouldn't be bored around here," he said, after a survey of the crowded section. "I've never seen such a heterogeneous collection of weird human specimens before."

"It's nice for dancing," she replied. "Shall we dance again?"

"Look!" He pointed at two negro wenches, in green low-cut dresses, their hair fluffed out like smoke furls, hoping to sidetrack her intention. "Two beauties, *n'est-ce pas?*"

He sniffed at them, sneered perhaps, but only because two women were dancing together. Mercado had no feeling against negroes.

Cléopâtre misunderstood him.

"You Americans," she said, "why do you hate the negroes? They are people like you and me. They can't help being black."

Mercado was piqued at the reflection on his lack of tolerance. He particularly prided himself on having no prejudices of that kind. Smiling quizzically, to conceal his resentment, he replied:

"I have often heard that you Russians hate the Jews."

"Jews!" she said, and looked dreamily at the polished thumbnail on her left hand. "But they're not people.

"I've killed many Jews," she added agreeably.

## CHAPTER SIX

MERCADO claimed afterwards that his first reaction to Cléopâtre's astounding remark had been a desire to laugh. As a matter of fact he never thought of laughing until an hour later. Even then his mirth was not an expression of amusement or gayety but consisted of a bitter painful chuckling which one holds in reserve for the moments one must laugh at oneself.

In the beginning he was stunned. He had to concentrate the faculties that remained in working order, on the immediate situation, so that the formalities, such as paying the bill and bidding Cléopâtre good night would be accomplished without exposing his agitation. He even held her in his arms on the ride back though, for all he felt, she might have been a feather bolster.

He had once watched a colony of ants perish in a hearth fire. They had been hibernating

in the trunk of a tree and had not awakened
while their home was being chopped into two-
foot lengths.   However, the warmth of the
fire, which was licking the walls of their domicile, aroused them from their lethargy.   Rush-
ing out of the one available exit they discovered
themselves on an island in a sea of flame. Some
ran wildly here and there, exploring their re-
maining terrain to the last inch.   Others kept
close to the hole from which they had issued,
occasionally diving down only to run out again
when the increasing heat warned them of their
imminent destruction.

A few, bolder than the rest, dropped from
the smoking bark, and were shriveled before
they had fallen on to the bed of incandescent
coals.

The scene kept rising in his mind.   Sometimes he likened the ants to Jews who were
being butchered as they fled from their flaming
houses.   Sometimes he was an ant, not knowing which way to turn in the conflagration that
threatened him.   His brain was too distraught
to criticize his mixed metaphors.   Besides, the
picture was not evoked by his will but seemed
to rise up before him of its own volition.

His great need, he felt, was some distraction which would postpone the time of reckoning. He feared sober thought would forbid further intercourse with Cléopâtre and never to see her again seemed a deprivation too terrible to be endured. On the other hand how could he kiss the blood from her lips?

To escape his thoughts he had the taxi stop as they were passing Zellis. He passed into the cabaret's bar which was deserted because of the lateness of the hour except for a few wobbly college boys from overseas and a handful of girls who had either been so unlucky as to have picked up no business or had finished work and returned for a bite to eat before retiring. He picked out one who he discovered was half Hindoo, half French, because her lovely classic features and dusky coloring would, he knew, have attracted him if his abnormal condition had not made him immune to female charm.

He bought her a drink and tried to get her chatting about her life. The subject was of unfailing interest to Mercado and he managed, by its aid, to throw off, for the moment, his agonizing preoccupation.

She was completely straightforward about herself and concealed neither her boredom nor the financial purpose that kept her up so late. As usual she had a child. . . .

Mercado, induced by a vague idea that making love would be a therapeutic measure, and having temporarily thrown off the inhibitions which would ordinarily have made him think twice before he acted, asked her to go out with him.

"And how much money will you give me?"

"A hundred francs."

"It is not enough," she said.

"It's all I have."

She shrugged her shoulders incredulously. Then, with a wan look, added: "If you wish it."

They went to the hotel next door and took a room. She immediately started removing her clothes. Mercado was taken aback by the baldness of her procedure and lost what little zest he had for the adventure. Yet her figure was more lovely than he had expected, and her tawny skin, as smooth and soft as the petals of a golden iris, gave him a thrill like that he received from the polished bronze bird of Brancusi.

But a statement he had heard, that eighty per cent of the French cocottes were unhealthy, most inopportunely came into his head. He had a great fear of the two widely advertised maladies, not having had sufficient experience in such matters to have become callous.

*"Vous n'êtes pas malade?"* he asked in laborious French, conscious that he should be saying thou instead.

The girl was extremely indignant. Her eyes blasted him. "You ask that?" she said. "It is for us to ask. We take our chances and ruin befalls us if we make a mistake. For you it is of no importance. For us it destroys our means of life."

Mercado apologized. There was nothing more to say. Contritely he removed his clothes. She lay passive, as if she were asleep, except for her dark large eyes which gazed quietly at the dingy chiffonier across the room. The mysterious resignation of the Oriental clothed her with dignity. Formal beauty sanctified her body. Mercado could not so much as touch her fingers.

"It is necessary," she said, "to know one another better. One cannot make love with a stranger."

Mercado made no comment and continued to keep his distance.

After a while she shivered slightly, turned her head so that her somber eyes shone upon his face, and asked:

"Are you satisfied?"

"Yes," he said, "I have always agreed with you but I am astonished that you agree with me."

"You will pay me without . . ."

"Yes," he said and rose to get his wallet.

She calmly dressed herself, took the hundred francs, and hoped she would see him again and that he would sleep well; all without the suggestion of a smile.

Mercado, however, had been helped by the interlude. He was able now to laugh at himself, laugh at the irony of fate which had caused him to become enamored with the one woman in the world whom he must, by every principle, hate.

The laughter, though it purged his mind, contracted his heart. He wanted the content of Cléopâtre's nearness, the warmth of her embrace. It was a new want. He had not known how lonely he had been until the necessity of leaving her forever made him envisage his former solitude. And yet the newness of the want did not prevent it from being more acute than any he had ever felt. Unappeasable throbs of emptiness made him turn over and over in his bed.

He must never see her again. If he saw her he could not keep himself from courting her without hurting himself more than he would by staying away. And it would be hideous to make love to the murderess of his kin. For a long while he saw no alternative.

Then a new train of thought slowly started to take form. Would it not be supremely just if he exposed the folly of her comprehensive hate by winning her love and revealing that he was one of the race she abhorred?

At this his heart rebounded, not because Mercado particularly relished the prospect of revenge but because such a procedure would permit him again to feel the pressure of her lips and to probe the mystery of her eyes. Perhaps to . . .

He checked himself. It was not the time to give way to voluptuous anticipations. The fibers of his racial consciousness vibrated. Jumping out of bed he paced nervously up and down the short length of his room.

He was a Jew. Her attitude rent the screen that hung between him and his ancestry. His mind hurtled back through the centuries. He stood, in vivid mental snapshots, beside Saul and David, the warrior kings. He served as a soldier under the Maccabees, fighting victoriously against stupendous odds. He manned a rampart at Jerusalem, while Titus, with the whole Roman Empire behind him, drove his cohorts to one assault after another. His race was not only a warrior race but the only ancient race of importance which had kept its virility down to his day. Poets, philosophers, scientists, prophets, musicians! And this charming blue-eyed creature had killed Jews because they were not people! He suddenly grew very tall. This sprig of a muddied upstart nation dared to be contemptuous of his people. Rather a joke on her. Too good to keep if her not knowing had not amused him.

He had always thought of himself as a

teacher of literature, drowsing through uneventful days in an American college town. All at once he was the last of a mighty race, courting a murderess who had tortured his brethren.

The teacher of English faded into air. In his place stood a proud arrogant man who gloried in emotions that would have horrified his former self. He felt himself growing bigger and bigger . . . he lived . . .

The momentary ebullience subsided as suddenly as it had surged up. He was a man, past his first youth, in love with a girl. What was the good of all this bother about ancestry? The breeds were all mixed up anyway. Rather than hurt her he would deny his inheritance. His forebears had fought and hated, loved and married. Now they were dead. What did they care what became of him?

Mercado sank into a chair and held his head. He could not think clearly. As soon as he inclined toward one view its opposite seemed more attractive. No decision was possible until he could calm his fever and think consecutively. He was getting nowhere and needed rest. Tomorrow he would persuade Halsey to go off with him, at least for a few days, and doubtless the peace of nature and the exertion of pushing a wheel, would bring back a more normal mentality. Meanwhile he must get some sleep. He lay down and tried to think of other things.

But his will did not prevail. He tossed in his bed cursing his temperament which had made him take Cléopâtre lightly so long as no obstacle stood between them, while now that she had revealed contempt for him as a person and hatred of the race to which he belonged, he perversely desired her more than his life.

It was ridiculous and degrading. He was nothing more than a fool who deserved everything that was coming to him. He damned her lips and her eyes. He indulged in febrile, sadistic eroticism. But nothing was of any use.

## CHAPTER SEVEN

MERCADO is one of those rare individuals who wake up in good humor. Even when an alarm clock routs him, his eyes open in a smile. Many a morning Halsey suffered in silence while his friend soniferously donned his trousers. Halsey liked to be quiet during the first hours of the day. His faculties required a certain peaceful interval in which to collect themselves and resume their proper coördination.

Therefore when he knocked about noon on Mercado's door to ask if he would join him for breakfast, and received in reply a surly: "No, I've had it," Halsey rightly inferred that something had gone wrong the night before.

Still he was not prepared for the peremptory tone Mercado adopted to announce that they were starting, that very day, on their excursion.

"Sudden, your decision?" he commented.

"Not so very," Mercado grunted.

"It seems to me I might have been consulted, considering that the trip was postponed on your account."

"Something has come up . . ."

"So I deduced."

Halsey waited for details which were not forthcoming.

"I told Vera I would meet her for tea," he added.

"Send her a pneumatic."

"Why the Hell should I?"

Then Halsey laughed. It was too ridiculous for them to quarrel like schoolboys. He recovered his equanimity and decided to accept the unrevealed necessity which was hurrying them off, on faith.

"What train shall we take?"

They reached Chaumont that afternoon, obtained their bicycles from the station master, and rode thirty arduous kilometers before supper. They were so exhausted that the primitive accommodations which they found in Montigny, proved exceedingly welcome. Mercado remained taciturn throughout the evening and listened to Halsey's attempts at humor with a supercilious smile. The latter's patience was severely tried.

The next day was an exaggerated repetition of the previous one. Their saddles had no springs. Their backs had rusty hinges. The condition of their leg muscles and of those epidermic areas in contact with the machine, may be left to the imagination. It was their worst day. Saint-Lour was reached by five o'clock.

However, as they limped over the ancient bridge that joined the two sections of the village, a triumphant spirit lifted Halsey far above his petty bodily disabilities, while a kind of second sight mellowed the stucco walls and tile roofs, the shaded streets and old-fashioned gardens, so that in whatever direction he looked, a picture of beauty rejoiced his spirit.

Even Mercado was not immune to the charm of the evening hour by the stream, as they sat over some old brandy before the composite café and billiard room. He became articulate, in his rebound from the physical concentration of the day, and revealed depths, to which, in their normal restrained living, Halsey had never penetrated.

In thinking it over, Halsey reflected that a friend of old standing tends to become part of one's familiar environment; he is accepted much as one accepts a favorite chair or the street on which one lives. To transcend the pleasant, uninspired monotony of such a friendship, an emotional disturbance is required. Thus their trivial quarrel led indirectly to a deeper understanding of each other.

Mercado first told the story of his last evening with Cléopâtre. He spoke eloquently, even describing his emotions, so that under the spell of his personality, Halsey lived vicariously through the peripatetics of that night.

Then they talked it over. Mercado had already worked out a theory to account for the apparent inconsistencies in Cléopâtre's character. He claimed she was essentially ordinary; not in the sense of common, just—not unusual. An ordinary person, he defined, is one whose reactions to life are governed by various external codes, and never by the exercise of their personal and peculiar mind. Of course, most men are, in this sense, ordinary.

Religions, patriotisms, ethical systems and standardized novels provide a large selection from which they are free to choose their feelings and ideas. Even their choice is often governed by the influence of some other person who dominates them and is dominated in turn by some one else. Society may be likened to an endless chain depending for its progress on a few real people, sports in the biological sense, who unless very careful, are outlawed. In the old days the "sports" normally rebelled against the current mythologies and were branded as heretics; nowadays, with ethics to the fore, they become artists or revolutionists rather than prophets.

Cléopâtre only seemed anomalous to them because the code, to which she subscribed, made a virtue of individuality and eccentricity. Thus her startling changes of mood were in reality no more indicative of her personality than the philosophy of success was the product of the average American's own mental processes.

"Very plausible," Halsey agreed, "but it does not account for her attractiveness."

"I don't pretend to be attracted only to biological or any other exceptions," Mercado replied. "In fact, I don't think I have ever known a feminine 'sport' in the biological sense. One does not need to account for attractions.

The *fatal women* of hearsay and history come, for the most part, under this heading."

He added that if either he or Halsey should ever come in contact with a female biological exception it would probably finish their university careers and end their usefulness to society. "Yet I'd take the chance," he finished.

"I should think," Halsey remarked, "that it was only then that we'd begin to be useful to society." Prophets, artists, revolutionists, who, if not they, had been useful, and who else?

"Oh, but meeting a female 'sport,'" Mercado said, "would not make us into male 'sports.' It would only ruin us for what we are. Cogs."

"You consider, John, that you and I are ordinary?" Halsey queried.

"Of course," Mercado answered, "though you and I, like most ordinary people, don't think so."

"In that case I don't see that it matters if Cléopâtre is one also."

"It does, though. She interested me because, in the beginning, I felt she was a real person. If you remember, I used those words to you after meeting her. What I meant was that I felt she might become a real person."

He went on to assert that naïveté and simplicity in youth were often portents of mature greatness. They implied that a person had refused the ready-made analyses of the world and waited, with open mind, for the lessons that experience would confer. But if he were wrong, if Cléopâtre was but ordinary, the intimacy which a mutual physical attraction brought in its train, would only make him familiar with the Russian average mentality. "And for that," he finished, "I've no use, though, I confess, a curiosity."

"Then you are going to see her again when you get back?" Halsey asked, impressed by his carefully worked out point of view and full of admiration for Mercado's detachment. Apparently he was uninfluenced by the racial issue.

"I think so," Mercado replied. "Naturally I've oversimplified the problem. There is no such thing as a person who is altogether real." Even the most ruthless intellects had their blind-spots; usually some phase of their traditional group viewpoint was taken over without its having undergone the critical scrutiny to which all other phenomena had been subjected. It was quite possible that Cléopâtre had intellectual integrity and emotional honesty toward everything but Jews.

"And there is still another aspect," he went on. "We assume that the wish to exterminate the Jews in Russia signifies an impolitic, barbaric and narrow-minded attitude. It is quite natural for me to assume this, yet, from the ideal point of view, it is not justifiable." One should, if one's theory was to hold water, formulate judgments only on the basis of knowledge. He said that he had, as a matter of fact, no special knowledge on this subject. He didn't know Russian Jews. He didn't know Russians. His condemnation of Cléopâtre's attitude was based entirely on racial prejudice.

"Come now," Halsey said, "that's a bit strong. We've both read history."

If history taught anything, it taught that the future of any particular race cannot be prognosticated. One never knew which branch of mankind would forge ahead and seize the what-you-may-call-it, the torch of progress. One had no more right to kill off Jews than to kill off Nordic blonds.

Mercado said that he agreed from a detached point of view. But Cléopâtre was not detached.

She was a Russian. It might be, at least he did not know if it was so or not, that it was essential for Russia to get rid of its Jews.

"What are you driving at?" Halsey was very puzzled.

"Only that Cléopâtre's ruthless anti-Semitism is not a sufficient cause in itself for me to condemn her."

"What more do you want?"

"I want to be convinced that her fondness for the exotic, her joy in danger, her absence of restraint, and the warmth of her feelings, are false. If I were sure that the face she presents to the world is an acquired, artificial pose, adopted because her milieu has stamped it with approval, I should lose all interest in her as a person and retain only the intellectual curiosity one has of foreigners."

Halsey let the subject drop. Later, when he had time to reflect upon Mercado's argument, he began to doubt if Mercado was as rational as he had pretended. If Cléopâtre had not attracted him physically, would his attitude have been so generous? Halsey shortly afterwards discovered that the matter had still another phase.

Plombières-les-Bains, Remiremont, Gerardmer. The meadows rolled by in long, slow curves. A little restless stream, which was continually crossing the road, cheered them with its company. A great wood received them, whose red columns, rising straight from the floor, raced speedily by, while the slender distant shafts, far back in the shadow, seemed hardly to move.

But though their physical aches were less importunate and their pedals turned over without requiring conscious effort, still a glorious feeling of relief thrilled their spirits when they finally reached Lake Longermer where they planned to spend the night. A real day's work, they felt, had been accomplished.

After tea they went for a swim.

"Sorry you came?" Mercado asked as they sat side by side on the strip of beach, drinking in the sounds and smells of the twilight.

Halsey thought of the rapturous transports he was sacrificing, of the ecstasy inherent in Vera's lips, of the wild exaltation that actuated their parties, but he answered: "No. A moment like this is worth far more than the artificial stimulation of the cabarets. It is natural and healthful. There is no let-down afterwards."

"Both have their values," Mercado sur-

[ 151 ]

prised Halsey by objecting. "If we are born into the world to feel we should not limit ourselves to the temperate pleasures."

Though the emotional side of Halsey echoed this sentiment, it conflicted with his ingrained ethical convictions. He had, partly for his own protection, to fight against it. He could not effectively plead morality; he believed morality was only accepted custom, so he countered by questioning Mercado's assumption.

"But are we born into the world to feel?" he demanded. In his opinion all that nature asked of them was that they propagate.

Mercado, a bit contemptuously, answered that he'd gone back to the problem of the chicken and the egg. If nature had only wanted life to reproduce, there would have been no need of elaborating the simple mechanism of the amœba. "No!" he exclaimed, "we are here to undergo every kind of emotion of which our nervous systems are capable. Only thus can we attain maturity. That is why I so eagerly followed up the impulse which drew me to Cléopâtre. And it has been worth while. I've experienced feelings which . . ."

"I don't see," Halsey was irritated and answered with some heat, "that what you went through differs radically from the usual sort of thing. Your theory makes miscegenation the most desirable union."

"Not at all." Mercado drew up his knees. His eyes were regarding the cup between two distant hills from which a bouquet of flamboyant clouds spiraled like flowers in a basalt vase. They had assumed an odd, abstracted look. His voice was low and very serious. He continued, slowly: "When Cléopâtre said to me, 'I've killed many Jews,' I wanted to laugh." He didn't know why. It wasn't because her words were funny. Her lips were still the lips of a good little girl. Her chin tilted coquettishly, her dark eyes sparkled. "Let us dance!" she had said, smiling up at him. "Dansons!"

The whine of the fox-trot, the rhythm of their bodies, the clover hay effluvium of her hair, visions of screeching, terror-stricken Jews fleeing before a mob . . . Mercado couldn't begin to describe his emotion. The only word that came to him was *chic*. Halsey knew what he meant. In the French sense. Something out of the ordinary, exclusive, esoteric. Her infant face lay confidingly in the hollow beneath his chin.

Her remark had shattered his complacency as a fire siren blasts a ship's midnight sleep. Though he was a pure-blooded Jew, he had just about forgotten it. He supposed it was because his family had not been religious for several generations and neither his looks nor his name denoted his race. Perhaps it was only natural that the fact of his Oriental origin should have dropped back into the dark corners of his consciousness . . .

"I imagine," Mercado went on after a long pause, "you think I'm inconsistent."

"Think!" Halsey exclaimed.

Mercado laughed. "In a sense you're right." Certainly the conclusions of his logical mind had little in common with the emotional blow-out to which he had just confessed. Yet this incongruity was normal, he believed, in humans. Intellect was a late arrival and often conflicted with the more instinctive and direct emotions.

Halsey refused to admit this. He claimed that the function of the intellect was to criticize, restrain, and coördinate the emotional stimuli. There was no conflict. The feelings

[ 154 ]

spur one on to act. The intellect passes on the advisability of the action. It was the last court of appeal and should hold the balance of power.

"What would you think of me," Mercado asked, "if I chose to curb my intellect and allow my emotions free scope? Because I found it amusing or satisfying."

"I would probably call you a fool." Halsey answered without hesitation.

Mercado acknowledged he would probably be right, yet he was tempted. The sensations of that night were, in a way, quite glorious. He had always been so logical, so sane, that it gave him a marvelous sense of liberation even to feel passionately, savagely . . . as for acting . . . well, he hadn't decided yet.

Halsey looked at him sharply. He, too, was tempted. He wondered if Mercado knew it, but concluded that his friend was too concerned about himself to indulge in extraneous speculations. He offered him the criticism which he had been directing against himself.

"Don't think," he said, "that you're becoming primitive. Your pleasure comes from watching, with your sophisticated mind, the antics of your Neolithic emotions."

Mercado replied that certainly there was something in his contention. Especially if he meant in retrospect. But it wasn't that at all at the time. "Have you ever," he asked, "lost your temper?"

"I suppose so," Halsey admitted.

"Did you enjoy it?"

"No," Halsey answered, for he remembered his ineffectual adolescent rebellions with a sense of shame.

"Well, I haven't lost mine since childhood, yet, unless I'm mistaken, there was a very definite kind of pleasure in letting the fur fly." Of course, he added, his outbreaks were always futile and as a result the misery of defeat immediately spoiled the fun; but if he had carried everything before him . . . he thought, really, there might be a lot in Cléopâtre's idea.

"Oh, so that's it!"

Mercado flushed with annoyance. Halsey was sorry he had spoken but there was no use trying to retract his remark. Besides it was probably pertinent, and it would be better for Mercado if he realized what lay behind his reasoned defense.

The next day they continued on their way.

Motor buses from Gerardmer began to over-
take them, filled with strange faces and headdresses, such as were drawn by Daumier. They
breathed easier after each bus had passed but
another inevitably followed. The quiet of the
forest was shattered. There was no more spar-
kle in the morning air. They were trudging up
a mountain, leading wheels that had to be
watched every moment, as they balked at the
slightest provocation and tangled themselves
up with their legs.

Though their turtle-like progress was dis-
couraging the Col de Schlucht was finally attained. From there they coasted at terrific
speed and in great danger of breaking their
necks into Colmar. The Rhine was still distant.
It was not until four o'clock that they reached
its brink, at a place called Sponeck, and rested
on the stone parapet which bounded the broad
fast river.

Both were worn out by fatigue. They
watched, for a while, in silence the changing
designs of the surface.

"I would like," Mercado suddenly remarked,
"to get back to Paris."

"I've been expecting it," Halsey replied in

a resigned voice, though as a matter of fact nothing, at that moment, would have suited him better.

"What do you mean?"

Halsey realized they were on the verge of a quarrel. Nerves are so easily rasped when one is tired. He quickly pulled himself together and explained he only meant that they were out of luck and exhausted. As they had been having a good time he thought it would be wiser not to make a decision until they had had a sleep. The Black Forest and Strasbourg were not far away. No doubt there was some town nearby where they could spend the night in comfort.

Mercado answered that if their choice lay between Paris and further bicycling, he would agree with him. "But there's more in it than that," he insisted. "I made up my mind yesterday. Of course, if you seriously object . . ."

"What is it?" Halsey asked though he had a pretty good idea of what was on his mind.

"I've decided to reform."

"By returning to Paris?"

"I've held, as long as I can remember, pretty

definite views on life and I've never tried them out. It is now or never."

"Aren't you taking a casual adventure a bit seriously?" His friend asked assuming he was referring to Cléopâtre.

Mercado answered that it wasn't the particular episode that mattered, it was the principle of the thing. He had a hunch that if he ducked under once more, because it was safer, he would spend the rest of his life mumbling over a golden oak desk into vacuous ears.

"And if you take up with Cléopâtre you'll . . .?"

"I don't know," Mercado said, "it's just a superstition I suppose . . . but I don't think it will be that."

"Of course," Halsey was a bit impatient, "I can't argue about magic with you."

"You consent to go back then?"

"I wish," Halsey obstinately replied, "not so much for my comfort or satisfaction, but because I think it would also clear your mind, that you would explain what you hope to accomplish before . . ."

"I can't do that. I don't hope to accomplish anything. I just want to see the thing through."

"You contemplate, I gather, a love affair with this gentle creature."

"I don't contemplate anything." Both were irritated. Halsey, controlling his voice so that it sounded superficially courteous, continued to cross-examine him. He blamed himself afterwards for not having minded his own business. He had been irascible owing to fatigue.

"You've evidently," he said, "swallowed the bait and been well hooked. On no other basis can I understand a man, whom I've known as intelligent, refusing to regard the possible outcome of an intended action. Excuse my impertinence in requesting information. I look forward to the dénouement with interest. Your taste, if I may use an expression of Cléopâtre's, is most original."

Mercado was furious. He started to speak but thought better of it. All at once he began to smile. "Bill," he said, "you must be scared to death of Vera. I had never thought of that. Don't worry, I'll take care of you."

Halsey was too astounded to more than sputter: "Vera, what about Vera?"

"Do you plan to see her again?" Mercado continued. "Hadn't you better keep away?

How are things progressing? You've never mentioned her."

The last thing Halsey wanted to discuss was Vera. "We've been having good times," he said, "but I attempt, in *my* relationships, to keep things in some kind of proper perspective."

He hadn't intended to emphasize the "my." Anyhow the words were spoken. Mercado took them as another rebuff and relapsed into silence. Halsey was sorry, but thought it best to let the matter drop. He was overcome by lassitude and they had to ride seven kilometers further to reach Markelsheim, the nearest city. To stay where they were was unthinkable. The house and garden were filthy.

They took the train the following morning and were busy changing cars most of the day. Neither of them felt like talking. Their little difference seemed to widen during the journey.

## CHAPTER EIGHT

THE coolness, which had originated on the banks of the Rhine, lasted for several days after their return. Halsey and Mercado remained ostensibly friendly, both having enough sense of proportion not to exaggerate a trifling difference. They even took their meals together, shared a double room, and chatted pleasantly about various matters of mutual unconcern. However, not until the insistence of Vera and Cléopâtre persuaded them to hire a rowboat in the Bois de Boulogne and pose, the four of them together, for a snapshot, was the old intimacy reëstablished. They felt so absurd before the camera that their stiffness was quite dissipated. After which they related their experiences to each other. Mercado felt a need for at least one person to whom he could open his mind. He suffered more than Halsey from the estrangement and was very pleased to resume the old relationship.

## THE PROFESSORS LIKE VODKA

Mercado had gone up to Montmartre on the night of his arrival. He had slipped behind one of the little tables near the bar and had ordered vodka, content, for the time being, to luxuriate in an atmosphere which became more congenial and less exotic each time he savored it.

He was not left entirely alone. The French girl, who acted as hostess, welcomed him back. The little English singer sat with him for a while and related the gossip of the establishment. The barkeeper surreptitiously made a caricature of him and sent it over to his table as a surprise. It wasn't half bad either.

As he expanded under the friendly camaraderie, he reflected that the Caveau was unique in its way. Its trade-mark might be, "Money extracted painlessly, victims cry for more." In no other place would he pay such exorbitant prices without rancor. One dollar and a half for cigarettes. Yet the girl was so persuasive with her basket and her smile, he could never resist just one package.

The first of his Russian friends to come upstairs was Liza. Even she looked good after Markelsheim. "Why did you not let us know you were coming? I fear," her oily smirk denied her regret, "Cléopâtre will not be able to join you. Such a shame. She is engaged downstairs. A rich Argentine. Good business. Much champagne."

Cats, Mercado reflected when he had got rid of her, are unjustly defamed when women are likened to them. Sometimes, it may be admitted, they are indifferent to their masters. Certain cats have been observed to fawn, when hungry, upon prospective benefactors and to exhibit the most obtuse apathy after their nutritive requirements have been satisfied. This is not, however, the rule. Those who have had the pleasure of a long, close intimacy with any respectable cat, will testify to the sincerity and amiability of the race. A cat, even when abruptly awakened from slumber by an awkward caress, will purr sweetly. This can be said of few women.

Though shamelessly neglected and left alone in an apartment during the whole day and the greater part of the night, when his master finally returns, drunk or sober, cheerful or sad, pussy will rub himself against his legs, bow, curtsy and express, by every gesture at his command, delight at the homecoming. Women, under similar circumstances, do not exhibit a like generosity. It was only natural that Cléopâtre, unaware of his premature return, should be attending to business. What else should she be doing?

Vera was shaking his hand. Her approach, as usual, had been startling. Her animated features, her gestures, breathlessly dramatic, made Mercado feel as if she had just run up a hill after him.

"Where is Bill? Why isn't he with you? Did you come back alone? Is he all right? Why didn't he come with you?"

Mercado, selecting the one question he could effectively answer, told Vera that they had returned together. Then he asked for Cléopâtre.

"I go to get her." Vera hurried abruptly away. "Decent but crazy," Mercado said to himself, "and very curious that she should appeal to such typical Americans as Hamilton and Bill. The attraction of opposites again."

"Vera told me you were here."

Her greeting was of a calm simplicity. He might have left her but fifteen minutes before.

Her only expression of pleasure was the one shy, happy glance that seemed to slip by accident from her demure eyes.

"I could not stay away any longer," Mercado answered, forgetting, for the moment, all about her Kooboy speech.

"You are alone?"

"Yes."

"You should have warned me. I must go back."

"It doesn't matter. I'm tired, been traveling all day. I just wanted to look at you."

Mercado, catching the soft note in his voice, chided himself. Such bad tactics! As usual the more he cared, the more stupidly he acted. Though burning with desire he must, to be successful, assume nonchalance. He should take his cue from Cléopâtre. Probably it was just her indifference which had bewitched him. Man always pines for that which eludes him while the ripe fruit beneath his hand may rot for all he cares. Were not indifference and repose the most effective weapons of offense in the battles of love?

He looked at Cléopâtre sitting silently across the table from him. Her repose, among such turbulent surroundings, for even the frescoes on the walls and the glasses on the tables had an uneasy, restless look about them, was so incongruous that she became, Mercado felt, by her very restraint the most conspicuous individual in the room. He compared her to the eye of a storm where everything is peaceful, the wind is still and a small circle of blue peers quietly down from above, while all around a pandemonium of motion, force and tumult mingle in chaotic confusion.

He desired to break it down, but did not know how. She would not drink with him. Her duties required her to drink with strangers. She was sick of it, but what could she do?

She had little to say for herself and seemed more interested in the details of his trip. After a while she got up to go.

"But when will I see you?" Mercado anxiously asked.

"Would you like to meet me at Fouquet's, day after to-morrow?"

"What about to-morrow?"

"Too busy." Mercado was grieved. He had curtailed his excursion only to see her. He was leaving for America in ten days.

"To-morrow," she said, "my brother arrives from Lyon. He will want to see me. Of course I am always here at night."

"Your brother," Mercado asked, "the one that killed your husband?"

"I have only one brother, but how is it you knew that?"

"You told me."

"How *drôle!* I do not remember."

"*Drôle!* But you never told me why."

"Do not speak of it," she said, giving him her hand and quietly moving away.

His zest went with her. Though aggrieved without cause, he could not argue himself out of it. A feeling of discouragement fuddled his sensations. He realized at last that he was very tired.

Having paid the bill he left without saying good night to any one. When he reached the entrance on the ground floor, the thought occurred to him that he had never seen the Caveau proper, where Cléopâtre and the other entertainers spent the early part of each evening. He went down the stairs and looked in. The room was more attractive, with its swinging lamps, than those above, but had no dancing floor. He noticed Cléopâtre. She was against the far wall, next to a man with sallow skin and a shining mustache. They were chatting. A glass of champagne lolled between her fingers. Liza caught sight of him and, being alone, started in his direction. Mercado slipped precipitately backward into a jingling Cossack and mutely fled.

The next day and night he spent by himself thinking, sometimes calmly, sometimes feverishly of Cléopâtre. When calm, he felt as he had on the bicycle trip, that she was an ordinary Russian bourgeoise, differing only in experience from the other thousands that had been brought up similarly. As the daughter of an army officer she would have absorbed, with her first words, moral verdicts which he, as an American, could not but hold shocking. The killing of enemies had doubtless always been in her eyes the most glamorous of pastimes and the murder of non-combatants a matter of inconsequence. As hatred of the Jews was universal among her people, the notion that another point of view was possible had probably never entered her head. Therefore how could he in fairness hold her accountable for a sentiment that she could not conceivably have avoided?

He could not. Which made his procedure clear enough. He would take from her whatever she had to give and think no more about the bloody specter of racial hatred hovering above them. She, unaware of its presence, would not be troubled by it. As for him, its ghostly breath added a poignancy to their little drama which seemed to raise it to the sublime level of classic tragedy. And yet it need not end tragically. That was the beauty of it.

Then he would pass, in imagination, through the various phases of courtship which prelude consummation. He took for granted his advances would be welcome, although such confidence was strange considering the little encouragement he had received. And when it was all over and they were lying side by side in that delicious peaceful state which makes one curse the progress of the minute hand, he would smile inside at the secret in his heart. At the four words he would not say. Instead he would kiss the tears from her eyes and go softly away leaving a memory. For a beautiful memory is a treasure ever after, while a shock, no matter

how violent, can not sever the roots of a fundamental bias. And why should he bring suffering, for no cause, to one who had given him
pleasure?

Such was the climax he foresaw when his
thinking was calm. But it was never calm for
long. The brother, of whom he knew but one
fact, had a knack of intruding on his reverie.
And his figure, mysterious, defiant, portentous,
made the blood run faster, worked up an excitement in him that broke down his detachment and awakened strange lusts. He did not
know why the brother caused so drastic a transformation in his mood. Many a brother had
killed a husband, sometimes by accident, sometimes in self-defense. And in any case it was
not a score for him to settle. On the contrary he should be grateful for the deed. Had
it not given him his opportunity?

Probably, Mercado decided during one of his
more rational moments, the brother subcon-
sciously affected his attitude toward Cléopâtre.
So long as she was alone in Paris, sole buffer
between an infant boy and the world, he had to
be considerate and kind. But with a brother,
and such a capable one, in the offing, she for-

feited the protection of his chivalrous code. She became forthwith a member of a clan, its representative, for had she not killed his people with her own hands?

Thus the brother's unseen presence transmuted their romantic friendship into a symbolic drama, and moved their affair out of the closet of a personal relationship onto a great public arena. It was then as if Mercado looked down from a height on two puppets, representing two ancient traditions, as they rushed toward the tragic climax which inevitably results when mortals assume the burden of immortal quarrels. He was to be the instrument of divine vengeance. The line of Saul and David had not run out. The Canaanites were still scourging the Chosen People.

Mercado felt he had a great part to play. The prospect filled him with rapture. Especially as he would be both spectator and protagonist. It seemed glorious to combine man's love of a woman, symbolic hate of a racial enemy, and fear, fear of the unknown (for who could tell the result of his confession?), in one inclusive, overwhelming emotion. Though each scene that led by measured inevitable steps up to the great climax would have its distinct dramatic effect, unique and interesting, Mercado anticipated, more than all the rest, the final tableaus. For it would be, in a sense, his scene. His voice, cloaked in the humility of a confession, would falter, feel its way, burdened by the prescience of what its message would destroy.

Such anticipatory emotions, though vivid enough—for they were less diluted than emotions inspired by an actual event—were not satisfying. They left an aftermath of futility. The hours passed slowly. He was impatient for the curtain to rise. He wanted to get Cléopâtre talking about Jews.

However, he resisted this desire until they had been together several hours. She was so placid. Evidently no suspicion of his inner turmoil had impinged upon her serenity. They had coffee and, after a pleasant stroll down the Champs-Elysées, went to dinner.

Afterwards, the night being unusually warm for Paris, they drove through the Bois.

"Let us go and sit by the lake," she said. "I adore the reflection of the moon on the water."

Mercado paid off the cab. They found a

spot by the shore, black as ebony, where a chestnut tree leaned over the water. Her cloak protected them from the dew while the grass beneath made a soft mattress for their bodies. No one was near and only the sound of the automobiles, up above on the highway, prevented a perfect illusion of isolation.

"Tell me," Mercado asked after a long kiss, while the moon delicately hid behind a cloud, "have you killed many Jews?"

"Yes," she said, "a great many." He had slipped his hand beneath the collar of her dress. A phrase, the music of the spheres, floated in and out of his reverie. The ensemble was perfect. The soft form, pressing so gently against him, was part of the summer night's magic spell. He was hampered by a pin with a trick catch.

"My father," she continued, "raised a band of Cossacks to serve under Denikine. We were only one hundred and fifty strong. I rode with them for a year and a half. They were a great band. Not one but had killed. We raided the towns behind the enemy's lines. I don't think a Bolshevik or a Jew was left alive in our path."

"Dear one," he said as he finally solved the

trick of the catch, "how did you know the Jews were Bolshevik?"

She pressed his hand. The silk of her dress and the velure of her skin held it immobile between them. He wanted to bury his face in the fragrance of her bosom.

"Oh, we never bothered about that," she said, "it didn't matter. In any case, the fewer Jews the better.

"You mustn't!" she exclaimed, and turned toward him, entwining his body in her arms. Somehow their lips met in so overpowering an embrace that their entities seemed to merge, physically, one into the other.

"Just how," he added when he had pulled himself together, "did you kill the Jews?"

"Sometimes," she replied, "we would tie them to a fence, pour oil on their hair, and banquet by torchlight.

"Sometimes we would bury them in the ground up to their necks. There were always rats. We would watch the Jews fighting off the rats with their teeth.

"John!" Her hand had ousted his from beneath her dress and was now caressing his shoulder and side, sending electric thrills

[ 175 ]

through his frame as it brushed, softly, the smooth skin of his body. "You are strong, John, you Americans have good muscles."

"Did you ever kill Jews with your own hands?" he asked.

"Often," she said. "I was famous for it. . . . Listen!"

It was a moment when all the motor cars in the park were hushed. An oar splashed on the lake. A laugh, so lovely it resembled the trill of a song bird, floated in from a phantom boat. There was no other sound except the orchestra of the insects, crickets and cicadas.

"It is like a Russian night," she said. "They would crucify some young man for me. I would put a dagger between my breasts, the point against his heart, and slowly embrace him. . . .

"Here!" She opened her bag, "is the knife I used. I always carry it with me." It seemed to reflect the shimmer of her eyes. Mercado recoiled; shocked for the moment by the straight, hard steel. But even its edge could not cut the impalpable cords which drew them toward each other.

"John," she added, caressing the curve of his

neck, gracing the classic contour lovingly with her fingers, "your throat reminds me of it."

Mercado knew then Cléopâtre was becoming fond of him. His heart leaped with joy. They embraced each other again.

It was *chic*, Mercado reflected, *rigolo*. Only French words were adequate.

Cléopâtre stared at the lake, her eyes rich with shadows. "What time is it?" she asked.

Having parted from Cléopâtre at the door of the Caveau, Mercado returned to the hotel. He had always been a bachelor and should have been habituated by then to the desolation of white sheets and shapeless pillows. Yet just because of his lack of experience, a long night in which soft arms would open to receive him whenever he awakened, seemed surpassingly wonderful. He rebelled against a fate that had made him choose, of all the women in the world to love, the one he must inevitably hate. *Chic*, no doubt it was, but chicness is no balm for an empty heart or an empty bed. He fell asleep at last worn out by self-commiseration.

In the morning his energy had returned. He saw Cléopâtre once more through normal eyes. The cool light dispelled the transforming glow which had made her so desirable. Gayly he looked forward to future developments.

Years before Halsey had resigned himself to a life in which women played a minor rôle. He continued to enjoy himself without a suspicion that his new friendship was more than a pleasant interlude in the steady well-charted current of his existence. Conscientious scruples did not bother him, for Vera had not only made it clear that she expected nothing more from him than the pleasure of the moment, but she had also accepted money with which, she said, she would buy herself a present. She wanted a token to remember him by when he was gone. However, the gift, so far as he knew, had never been purchased and he carefully refrained from reminding her of the intention.

As a matter of fact, Vera was proving far too costly. Not only did she continually ask for champagne, which, according to her, she had always had in Russia so that no meal seemed complete without it, but she insisted on the most extravagant tips whenever they left a Russian establishment. The waiter, cloak-room girl, wine boy, even the manager and the doorman were always old acquaintances who must be looked after or they would consider her ungenerous.

"We are like that, we Russians," she told Halsey, "whatever any of us has, belongs to all the others."

He admired their solidarity, but would not have been insulted if his participation had been declined. With it all, her fondness for him was so obvious that he could not take offense at her conduct no matter how inconvenient it happened to be.

Besides, her attitude let him out of all responsibility. He could leave her, whenever he wished, without a qualm. While as for Mercado, if Cléopâtre should happen to care for him, he would not only find it painful to say farewell, but would suffer remorse for his behavior. And remorse has sometimes the disagreeable habit of lingering through the years.

Yes; he was the better off. Still it did not seem quite just that the money he had put aside by tutoring during his summer vacations should be squandered on strangers, while the easily-come-by inheritance of Mercado should be faithfully guarded by Cléopâtre.

However, such petty thoughts never troubled him after his second drink, and the physical responsiveness of Vera remained a perpetual wonder. He loved to kiss the nape of her neck and feel her quiver at the touch of his lips. It made him proud of his virility. She was more than willing to go further. In fact, she told him she had just moved into a new apartment with a woman friend, and that the friend was away in the country. Would he not let her prepare a home dinner, for he could not know from restaurant fare how good Russian cooking really was. Something held Halsey back, though he was tempted and not by the thought of food. He feared, he would not have called it fear, to be alone in a room with Vera. So long as they stayed in public places he was in control.

Vera also suggested that the four of them spend the week-end at a roadhouse on the Seine. Mercado greeted the proposal enthusiastically. Halsey, for a moment, thought he was going to be overwhelmed. He could not bear to be put in the position of a killjoy. But unexpected support came from Cléopâtre and one more crisis was safely passed.

In small things no one could have been more acquiescent. Whatever Vera, or Mercado for that matter, wanted, he was willing.

"We must," Vera announced when the four of them were together, "at least have our pictures taken before you go."

Halsey was astonished. He thought this kind of sentimentality was an American product, but he said:

"I'd love to, I'm so glad you thought of it. Do you know a photographer?"

"I've often seen one," she said, "on the lake in the Bois."

"It will be lovely," Cléopâtre added with enthusiasm. "We can all go for a row. I love to row."

Mercado objected. He dreaded an undertaking that might make him look ridiculous.

"What's the good?" he said, "my memory will be a far better record of our good times than an impossible picture."

"No! No! No!"

Grudgingly he acceded to their wishes.

The next afternoon they hired a boat. Halsey offered to row. They moved down the

[ 181 ]

small pond, passing other similar boatloads who sometimes waved and sometimes paid no attention whatsoever. After a while Mercado lost his self-consciousness and began to enjoy the novel sensation. An artificial waterfall tumbled into the lake at the lower end. Halsey was directed to pull the boat up close so that Vera and Cléopâtre could bathe their hands. They were so simple about it that the professors rather envied them.

Afterwards Cléopâtre took the oars, bending her back sturdily and forcing the heavily laden boat through the water at a good speed. Vera kept a sharp look-out for the photographer.

He was discovered at last under a tall red tree. He greeted their proposal with enthusiasm. A small crowd collected to watch the proceedings. With much fussiness he made them alter their pose again and again. Mercado was embarrassed. He tried to hide it under a sheepish grin. When the ordeal was finally over he was so relieved that he opened up at last. After a few drinks, the two friends were exchanging confidences as of old.

"I can't make them out," he said, "imagine wanting a picture of four poor fools in a boat."

"But don't you see," Halsey answered, "that's just what they do want. All this Caveau business is work for them. They dream of a good bourgeois life."

"Banditry in Mexico. No. You can't make the corners fit. One thing or another, but not both."

"I wouldn't be surprised," Halsey said, "if Villa liked to have his picture taken."

This notion impressed Mercado. He had no further comment to make, but started recounting what had happened to him since his return.

## CHAPTER NINE

"WHY didn't you take her up?" Mercado suddenly demanded, the day after they had their pictures taken. Halsey and he had been musing over a glass of coffee on the terrace of the Select. Observing that his friend was mystified by the question, Mercado added: "I know an inn on an island in the Seine. The building stands alone. Grapevines and creepers are strung between its windows. Apple trees in ordered ranks guard the approaches from the river. Wake up, Bill! Don't you remember Vera's suggestion?"

"That we go away for the week-end?"

"Of course. What are you made of, anyway?"

"Well, I haven't forgotten it."

"But you refused to go. I could have brought Cléopâtre round."

"It sounds great," Halsey admitted. "I must confess I was tempted."

"St. Anthony!"

"If one could segregate," Halsey went on unperturbed, "a couple of days from the rest of life, I could not have resisted. As it is . . ."

"Are you afraid?" Mercado impatiently cut in, "that it would be too hard on you to leave Vera afterwards?"

"Not exactly." Halsey stirred his coffee evasively. "That is only one possibility."

"We evidently are votaries of opposite systems."

Mercardo thrummed the table nervously with his fingers. He supposed he had no more right to try and convert Halsey to his system than Halsey had to convert him to his. Still he would be curious to hear the reasons. His own situation was much more precarious, yet his instructions were full speed ahead.

Halsey reluctantly complied, for he felt it was up to him to attempt an answer after the free way Mercado had been confiding in him. In life, he said, every action has its results. A truism. He believed that when one had time to contemplate an action before its inception, one morally bound oneself to see the action through. And he was not prepared to see the possible consequences of a sentimental idyll with Vera, through. That was all.

Mercado checked a blasphemous exclamation.

"How do you know she is?" he demanded.

"Her possible frivolity does not let me out."

"I'd like to know why it doesn't?" Mercado said. "It was her suggestion, not yours."

"Blame it on my inherited Puritanism if you like, John." Halsey spoke with an irritating patience.

Mercado said he was quibbling. That inhibitions were not inherited, they were acquired. Then he hesitated, and, having evidently decided to change his tactics, continued in the level conciliatory voice which he often used in the classroom.

He thought he understood what Halsey meant. He liked Vera too much to treat her as a cocotte, and not enough to consider marriage. Therefore, he did nothing but nourish her every evening and take of her afterwards what limited pleasure the swaying of a taxi would permit. "It's cutting things fine, to my mind," he said dryly, "but I suppose it's what the world calls sensible."

"That's it exactly."

Halsey was annoyed because Mercado bracketed his problem so cavalierly, but did not want to quarrel with him again. He tried instead to shift the subject, as he found it much easier to talk about Mercado's affairs than his own.

"Anyway," he added after a tense pause, "I don't see why my reluctance need hinder you in any way."

"I shan't let it," Mercado answered, somewhat mollified. "But it would have been nice if the four of us could have gone off together. We have been having good times and I like to feel you somewhere near."

"Getting a bit nervous about the mysterious brother?" Halsey asked with a laugh.

Mercado took the question seriously and thought for some moments before replying.

"I'm not nervous," he finally said, "but I'm in rather a quandary." He spoke softly as if he were addressing an inner tribunal rather than the friend he had just been gibing. Halsey was glad he had not spoken more sharply. "The trouble is that I'm so damned happy when I'm with Cléopâtre that old dreams, which I thought my mature cynicism had permanently incarcerated, have come to life and confused my intentions. You know the sort. We all tinker with them when young. About every man and woman having a predestined mate who, if found, can be loved ever after. The real thing, you know. Eternal, complete in itself, and all that. When I'm with this little Russian creature and our eyes meet or our hands touch, nothing seems to have reality but the feelings of the moment. All my intellectual skepticism and my well-founded doubts are washed clean away. It seems like insanity to imperil the wonder we bring to each other for anything so trivial as past events. Only the present, after all, matters."

He went on to say that it had become so bad he was obsessed by her even during the day. He couldn't get her out of his mind as he used to, but wondered with whom she was, and what she was doing. If she was thinking of him and longing, as anxiously as himself, for their next meeting. She had introduced him to a blond youth, a Russian, whom she called one of her best friends. Actually he was jealous. He had

[ 188 ]

a strong desire to murder the youth, just because he was able to talk with her in a tongue he could not understand.

Halsey would have been amused by this confession if Mercado had not been so upset. His infatuation had evidently been intensified by the complexities of the situation. He was leaning his chin on his hands and spoke with a meekness and gravity that were new to Halsey. In order to sound him out on the eventuality which his condition suggested, Halsey asked why he didn't drop all this rubbish about revenge and marry the girl. She would enliven the social life of the college and would probably make a most domestic wife in the bargain.

Mercado turned his glowing brown eyes on his friend and demanded if he were serious.

"Of course!" Halsey replied. Leaving out the personal equation which was his own exclusive problem, he thought the faculty wives would fall for Cléopâtre like a pack of cards. Instinctively they realized their need for new blood. None of them would be able to resist a Russian exile. The very word connoted romance and that they longed for more than anything, secret readers of the *Saturday Eve-*

*ning Post,* the lot of them. He could see Cléopâtre walking by the Commons with every window spotted by undergraduate heads, whisper-
ing to each other: "There she goes." Mercado's classes would become the most popular
on the curriculum.

"It would be diverting," Mercado suggested,
"to have her remark, at one of Mrs. Smith's
teas, after a sigh: 'Such a quiet life! I'm getting restless. Let's join the Ku Klux Klan
and tar a few Jews!' "

Though Halsey felt this remark hardly deserved a serious answer he replied that by the
time she knew enough English for that, she
would know enough about conditions not to
say it.

Mercado suddenly became animated.

"Look here," he said, "are you honestly ad-
vising a marriage based on a lie? Don't you
realize the step is far too serious to treat
lightly?" They were too old to be frivolous
about matrimony. Halsey evidently didn't
realize the hold her old life had upon her. She
got more fun killing than from any other diversion. At least so she had contended in a long
argument with him the other day. She claimed

it was merely a question of what one was used to and that under similar circumstances he would have developed the same tastes.

"Are you sure," Halsey asked, "her blood-thirstiness isn't just *chichi?*" He had the impression that what she really wanted was a home and security.

Mercado didn't know, but he did know that he was not going to take her across the sea without telling her who and what he was. And he also knew that when she learned he was a Jew she was not going to marry him, even though she didn't try to kill him. "Such things go deeper than you think," he added, "and then, there's the brother."

"Whom you'll probably end by making a friend of," said Halsey.

"But I don't want the mother of my children to be a Jew hater."

Halsey was beginning to get weary of the discussion. "Do what you think best," he said, "but, if you're not going to marry her, don't tell her who you are."

"And why not?"

"She may have become fond of you."

"In which case I should just desert her, giving no reason, and let her think me a cad ever after."

"That would probably be more agreeable to her than to think she had fallen in love with a Jew," Halsey answered. Besides, he didn't imagine she banked very heavily on his constancy.

"She doesn't believe in it at all. She thinks I'm playing with her," Mercado admitted.

"We'll leave it at that." Halsey was irritating.

"I'll be damned if I will," Mercado shouted. "Either she's worth while or she's a nonentity, and I'm going to find out which."

Mercado's vehemence made Halsey realize the futility of further conversation. The time for words was past. His rôle was to watch the course of events and finally to take his friend home. He congratulated himself on his own prudence. Mercado's condition was none too happy. His feelings were tearing him apart. He still wanted to talk and Halsey decided not to interrupt as he felt they were likely to quarrel and Mercado might need him badly in the near future.

"I've thought about this," Mercado went on

to say, "a great deal more than you suppose." He believed he saw it all pretty clearly. Essentially it was a conflict between two opposing forces. The first was an affection between a man and woman, one of those strange inexplicable attractions, without logic or rational basis, which spring up unexpectedly, where least looked for, and sweep the convictions of a lifetime into the rubbish heap.

He had always felt that such affections had something of the miraculous in their nature. Little yellow dogs changed into lions. Insignificant gray sparrows acquired the plumage of pheasants overnight. One was so accustomed to these transformations that one tended to take them for granted and merely smile, saying: "He has fallen in love," having reduced the only miracle to a formula.

The other force was also powerful. Its roots went back through antiquity to the unfathomable mists of prehistoric ages. It was the force which had sustained that ancient conflict which one may call, for convenience, the battle of Jew and Gentile, though as a matter of fact the division did not follow racial lines. The clash was really between mystic and realist, between the pursuer of intangible values and the man of so-called common sense. At times the battle had been to the death, at times an ostensible truce prevailed and each side made use of the achievements of the other. So it was to-day. The manufacturer of chewing gum utilizes the discoveries of the abstract scientist who seeks that most unsaleable of products, the truth.

But between Cléopâtre and himself there could be no truce. Her training demanded war to the death. The world, in her eyes, was a study in black and white. Jews were contemptible, despicable, iniquitous. There were no exceptions. To kill them was a virtue as well as a pleasure. She had never shaken hands with a Jew, she said. Did Halsey realize what that meant to him?

On his side he could not work up any blood lust. He had heard it was impossible for a Jew, but the Old Testament did not support this statement. Nevertheless his feelings were no less intense. His race, his kind of mind, was spat upon by a barbarian who possessed the virtues of an animal and the vices of man. He did not hate her, one does not hate someone beneath him, but he could not merely shrug his shoulders and observe her character with interest because of the other element: the desire.

Either love or hatred must carry the day. The only way to obtain a decision was to bring the two forces into the light. This he intended to do. Probably he would be hurt. His heart would be wounded, but in any case the result would give his mind much to ponder over. It was far too late to retreat.

Mercado's voice, which trembled as he made his points, and the curious glitter in his eyes denied the intellectual detachment to which he still pretended. He was evidently overwrought. Halsey felt that heroics, such as he contemplated, were both futile and dangerous. That he created a lot of pother about nothing at all. But protests would have been to no avail so Halsey refrained from making them. Instead he said:

"Let me know where you are if you leave town, and telephone me in case of need. I don't approve, but that doesn't matter."

"Thanks, old man," Mercado said, "I know you'll be there."

And then after a pause: "I don't think I'm

really in love with the girl. I do not consider passion, without respect, can properly be called love and in my case there is not even passion. That is, I am not at all obsessed by desire. I suppose some strange species of infatuation, like an exotic disease, has taken hold of me. Anyway I'm fully determined to go through with the thing for the reasons I gave you on the bicycle trip. If I turned back now the rest of my days would be filled with . . ."

His words ceased abruptly. Halsey looked round to see what had caught his attention. They were sitting in one of the cafés of the quarter much patronized by Americans. Many of their acquaintances had passed in and out, restlessly seeking, as is the custom over there, for nothing in particular. A girl, whom they knew only as the younger sister of one of their friends at home, had been sitting at the bar with a rather frowsy woman, drinking heavily as was her habit. They seemed overfriendly, but such is often the influence of liquor. The professors were used to the sight and paid no attention, though on their first days they had often wondered what her sedate married sister would have thought if she could have seen her.

A Frenchwoman, one of the short, business-like cocottes, had just entered and was vehemently berating their American acquaintance who seemed too befuddled to understand, and grinned foolishly and apologetically into her tumbler. The Frenchwoman's voice had become so shrill that all conversation ceased and every eye was turned in their direction.

Suddenly, without warning, the cocotte's small fat arm shot swiftly out, caught the American girl on the ear, and knocked her off the high stool on which she had been sitting. She lay full length on the floor, weeping.

Halsey and Mercado jumped up but were too far from the scene of action to interfere. Some one helped the long prostrate figure to its feet. Her hat had rolled under the bar. Her short hair was in her eyes.

The Frenchwoman began cursing again. Mercado managed to get the drift. Between strings of filthy abuse she repeatedly threatened, unless she came home immediately, to break her *gueule*. The American shrugged her shoulders deprecatingly. Some one handed over the hat. She put it on. Then, as if it had been her intention from the beginning, she got up and

[ 197 ]

stumbled out to a taxi, assisted by her recent assailant.

"I admit," Mercado continued, "that your system, founded on the maxim, 'Look before you leap,' is much safer. It is curious that in all that concerns the emotions, Americans of the old stock tend to follow the cautious philosophy of Benjamin Franklin, while in matters of finance, no group of people have been more daring and visionary. I suppose the much abused word, compensation, explains the apparent inconsistency. But we poor college professors cannot appease our emotional poverty by the gambler's thrill. Which may account for the fantastic pettiness of Faculty meetings.

"Anyway, unless Cléopâtre prevents me, I'm going to end this vacation with a flourish. Afterwards . . . who knows?"

They left it at that.

## CHAPTER TEN

CLEOPATRE paused on the second step and said, just as if it were a mere matter of course: "We *will go* to the country for the week-end." Then she hurried off without deigning to look at him again.

Mercado, completely taken aback, watched her bedraggled outline pass up the stairs and disappear.

They had been sitting on a bench in the Bois. A black cloud had risen in the west. Carelessly he had remarked that he hoped to cross the Atlantic before the equinoctial storms set in. But by the look of that . . . and he had pointed at the threatening cumulus.

He had stopped speaking. Something was happening to Cléopâtre. Not even her pupils had dilated, but he needed no visible sign to make him aware of her inner turmoil.

It had taken him completely by surprise. She had, up till then, maintained a mastery of her emotions which seemed impregnable. He had not even been sure she cared for him.

It must be the thought of his departure. Perhaps she had not realized that the moment to say good-by was so near. Perhaps she had not believed . . .

Hesitating, he had looked at her and asked: "What is it?"

"You are really going?" she said.

"But there has never been a question." He was mildly irritated. Surely he had not, by a single word, led her to think he would postpone the day.

"You are going to leave me here?"

"Where else?" His voice was a little hard, for the long-deferred victory came after days of suppressed suspense.

"Then you are really going?" Not a muscle twitched. She had the immobility of an Egyptian statue. Only the tear, which formed in each eye, and rolled down her cheek, confirmed his intuitive perception of her suffering.

"Look here," he said, "you've known it all along. It's nothing new." He tried to take her hand. She flung his arm roughly aside. He regretted they were not alone. Here in

the park . . . If only she would relieve herself by crying. Her repression terrified him.

She said nothing. She did not move.

He asked her why she took a temporary parting so tragically? If their bond was so strong
. . . if their love not only bore up but grew
greater . . . if they became more real to each
other when they were separated, a way would
be found, must be found, to unite them for all
time. One did not cast away the only treasure
life ever offered.

She did not stir. "Words! Words! Words!"
her silence shouted.

He made a move toward her but was checked
by something in her attitude. He felt she was
thinking: "Americans are fools. They do not
know enough to know whether or not they
love."

He tried to answer the unspoken thought by
more words. She should understand . . . life
was not so simple. He was poor. Dependent
on his job. Arrangements took time. When
love was real, time did not matter.

She got up and started walking very fast.
He followed. She entered the wood, turned
several corners, making no sign that she was

aware of his attendance. They reached a bridge over a motor road.

"Go away!" She turned fiercely upon him. "Leave me alone. I don't want you near me."

"I can't leave you this way."

He tried to soothe her by a caress. She knocked his hand down. He walked in silence, crediting her with the most horrible intentions. She looked capable of flinging herself over the rail.

He tried words again, there was nothing else, and he had to do something.

"This is no way to part," he said, "after what we've had together."

Then, encouraged by the sound of his voice, he pretended to be indignant. "You asked for a *camarade*. I have been one. You cannot expect a *camarade* to throw his life-work away for a whim"; weakly adding, "Don't be foolish."

"Idiot!"

She stared across the parapet while the rain-clouds slowly spread themselves over the sky and big drops began to spatter the pavement beside them. Soon the rain was falling in slanting filaments that looked, against the dark sky, like shading in an old line-drawing.

The water ran down his legs and squirted from his shoes when he shifted his weight. A miniature pond formed in the basin of his hat and flowed over whenever he turned his head. Cléopâtre paid no more attention to the rain than to him. It became darker and darker.

Was the miserable vigil ever going to end? He would probably catch cold. His throat felt scratchy already. And he had no idea what she would do next. She couldn't remain here forever. It must be getting late.

He fingered his watch but decided not to look at it. The dial would be invisible and he could never hold a match in this downpour.

What a mess! Russians! But there was nothing for him to do but to stick it out.

It became completely dark. Night must have fallen. Only the park lights, yellow blurs in the mist, were to be seen. He stayed close beside her, fearing she would slip away without his noticing it.

Just as he had given up hope and was reconciling himself to spending the night in the open, he felt her hand clutch his arm.

"Take me home," she said.

Eventually they reached the Porte Maillot

by a vague, timeless, wearisome effort, their feet dragging and their clothes making squashing noises as they moved their limbs. A taxi, fortunately, was at hand.

They finally got to her hotel. It was then she announced:

"We *will go* to the country for the week-end."

She was gone.

He waited a while, hoping for some further sign. The concierge looked at him curiously. There was nothing more to be done. Wet and miserable, he could only return to his room.

Mercado spent a restless night with a bandage round his neck. He swallowed two hot whisky-lemonades in short gulps, while his thoughts took a new direction. The subjective problems, which had obsessed him, became relatively unimportant. Abstract questions of conduct, the conflict between personal affection and racial antipathy, were no longer matter of pressing concern. He was in contact with a new and unexpected force which made his former emotions seem dilettanteish. Though they had been as real as any he had ever experienced, he could hardly recall them to mind.

Why did she wish to spend the week-end with him? His mind whirled about this question, once, twice, a thousand times throughout the night.

Had she worked out a scheme to entangle him so that if he remained obdurate she could force his hand? It sounded plausible in theory, but there were practical difficulties. The country being France, no law would be broken, nor did a night together in a hotel give her any hold over him. Perhaps the brother would be introduced at the critical moment and attempt coercion or blackmail. But if so crude a plan was in her mind, he had completely misinterpreted her feelings, and mistaken pique for wounded love. Mercado could not believe he had been taken in to this extent.

Another possible solution was that she hoped, by spending two nights alone with him, to seal the bonds of their affection; believing, in the optimism of her love, that he would not afterwards have the strength to leave her no matter what the cost might be. Mercado inclined toward this supposition, only distrusting it because it flattered him. It was gambling on a big scale; but Russians are renowned gamblers.

And the stake, after all, was not so great. What had she, a widow, to lose?

It also occurred to him that she might contemplate some obscure kind of revenge, either by making him ridiculous, or by making him suffer. But he could not figure out how she hoped to accomplish such ends. The means were too obscure. He finally dismissed the first and third hypotheses chiefly because he was convinced, from her conduct in the park, that she was fond of him.

It was strange how the dramatic assurance that she cared altered the complexion of their relationship. He supposed the uncertainty as to whether or not his affection was reciprocated had been preying on his mind without his knowing it. He had concealed it even from himself, although it must have had an influence, for now an entirely different set of anxieties harassed him.

Up till then he had hardly thought about the eventuality of her accepting him after she had learned who he was. The odds against it were so tremendous that its consideration seemed a waste of time. Now, it was not only possible, but probable.

He rose and looked out the window. The rain had ceased. Perhaps it was a good omen. To-morrow promised to be fair, for a yellow moon was peering over the chimney-pots of the house across the street. The city was asleep. He must get to bed. Mechanically he crawled between the covers.

What should he do under the circumstances? Marry her in Paris and bring her, as his bride, back to the university? Install her in his bachelor apartment and set up housekeeping? There was barely enough money for two; they would have to scrape and save. The prospect was absurd. He could not picture Cléopâtre buying groceries and picking out choice cuts of beef. Nor receiving in his sitting-room the formal calls of Mrs. Horace P. Smith, and serving tea while the visitor announced that there were seven speak-easies in the town, and immoral women, and my dear, the police would do nothing about it . . . *nothing!* The picture was impossible. Cléopâtre belonged to another world.

Besides, did he want to marry? Was he not too deeply rooted in the ways of a bachelor? It was terrifying to think of a routine which would compel him to return home for each meal and to explain every absence. And it would be worse than if he married an American, since Cléopâtre, in a strange land among an inscrutable people, would depend on him entirely. Everything would be different, the most trifling details, even. Neither of them would be happy.

Would she want a child? They could not afford one, not on his salary, but he was fascinated by the idea. The welding of two such opposite characters would insure an interesting offspring. If her strength and single-mindedness and his analytical brain were combined in one individual, the result could not help being formidable. And he would like to be the father of a remarkable son. Of course one could never be sure. The blood-lust of the mother and the instability of the father were just as likely to be the qualities inherited, and such a person would surely end in jail. Anyway, as they could not have children, the question was purely theoretical. She had a son already whose stepfather he would automatically become. A nice prospect that! He would be a fine father for a Russian boy.

"No; marriage is unthinkable."

Yet she bore a gift he prized above all things. The pettiness of life was sublimated when he was with her, each moment was ecstatic. If he cast away this gift, now that it was in his grasp, he would never forgive himself. Also, he had committed himself in advance. He was bound to see the adventure through. A backdown now would prove him despicably irresolute. He would even lose his self-respect. One can accomplish nothing if one shifts, like a weathercock, at every breath. As a matter of fact their prospects were no different from what they had been yesterday. It was only some peculiarity in himself that made them seem so. He must get some sleep . . . and he began to count, uselessly, "one sheep jumped over the fence . . . two sheep jumped over the fence . . ."

A flat-bottomed ferry-boat, attached to a cable, carried them over to the island.

"*C'est très sympathique, ici!*" Cléopâtre remarked, as they sat by the edge of the stream sipping their apéritifs. "You will think of it often, John, when you are far away."

"I shall throw a sou into the current," he said, "which will insure my coming back."

"To come back," she said, "is sadder than to stay away forever."

Her words depressed him. The sadness of the world sighed upward from the river in the form of spidery mist.

"How do you know so much?" he asked, attempting to be flippant.

"I don't know much," she said; "you know more than I do. But that which I know, I know."

Her confidence impressed him as an augury impressed an ancient Roman. What she said must, he felt, be so. His critical faculty was dormant before her downright statements. He would believe anything she said if it were presented with conviction, and Cléopâtre's ideas, unlike his own, were never tentative.

"Then," he replied, "this will be a very sad week-end."

"For you," she said, "perhaps. For me, life is finished."

"In that case my going away is nothing to you. Why did you complain yesterday?"

"One forgets, sometimes, for a moment."

Mercado watched a branch, floating down the stream, submerged, except for a single twig, which flaunted one red leaf above the water. Were his eyes really moist? The loveliness of the scene, the reflection of the apple trees on the water, the softness of the meadows across the river, gave him no pleasure. Loveliness, when one's heart is heavy, is an insult. As if nature were showing her contempt and indifference of man. Mercado felt he would never be happy again.

"It is beautiful, John, I am glad you brought me here. I am another person in the country. Perhaps you will like me better. I can understand that no one could love me in town. I am so miserable. Always I have the thought of my work which I detest."

"But I have loved you in town."

"No, John, not love."

She smiled happily, tipping her hat back so that she looked like a little country girl. Her eyes seemed to have lost their shyness.

"Let's go upstairs. I want to see our room."

Mercado stood by the open window. A round bed of flowers had been dropped in the middle of the lawn, like stewed red plums in a green bowl. Cléopâtre was unpacking her things behind him in the shadowy, high-ceiled room. He heard the rustle of her dress as she moved about. He knew her long lashes were wet with tears which never fell and never disappeared.

It is curious, he reflected, how certain moments stand out from the stream of time. The lengthening evening shadows, the barely audible voices calling from the river, and the fragile emotion which suffuses everything with its light. . . . The moment was rich with a thousand meanings, none of which he understood or wished to understand. It was enough to sink his eyes in the round bed of flowers, of a slowly deepening red.

She called him to her. "Hereafter," she said, "let us *tutoyer* each other. Let us call each other thou. I have heard that in English one says thou only to God. I like that. It must mean something to you. Let us *tutoyer* each other. Then, for me, there will be my son, my father, my brother, God and thou, my well-loved."

He kissed her. He did not feel her lips, for tears were in his eyes. He could not speak.

In order to regain composure he returned to the window and tried to impress the unfamiliar second person on his mind. He had never used it before. Twilight had quickly fallen and the crimson flowers had turned to black.

They ate dinner under the sky by the river's edge. Frogs were singing across the way, and now and again an invisible gudgeon jumped from the water, falling back with a little splash. A series of concentric ripples widened, and the moon drew golden lines along their crests. Each dish was better than the last. And the old Burgundy, which the waiter had ceremoniously decanted, had the fragrance of grapes and the sun. Though they mentioned the excellence of the cooking, they did not taste it. Their sensation, nourished on such impalpable stuff as the luster of eyes and the velvet touch of fingers, permitted no distraction. Mercado forgot to think.

Then they strolled, arm-in-arm, over their limited domain. It was dark beneath the apple trees, and the smell of the fruit harmonized with the fresh fragrance of her body. To feel her undulating movements, to see nothing but black leaves against a silver sky . . .

Afterwards they went upstairs, and Mercado stood on the balcony outside the window while Cléopâtre made ready for bed. He liked the matter-of-fact way she accepted the situation. No false modesty or feigned reluctance took away from the beautiful simplicity of their communion. To spend the night together seemed the most natural thing. He was a man, she a woman: in each other they found pleasure. The air was soft on his forehead, the frogs were quavering, the faint breeze, which lifted the window curtains, carried the scent of apples. He heard her voice . . .

They made love.

Mercado, in telling about it, surprised Halsey by his lack of self-consciousness and by the candor of his comment. He seemed unaware that one doesn't talk about one's inner emotions, that convention rules it isn't done. His voice was as quiet and unperturbed as if he were lecturing on Edgar Allan Poe.

"We made love. Three simple words and

yet what a gamut of sensation they include! Making love may mean so little, a physical act, pleasant or unpleasant, but no more important than the other routine performances of our bodies. Or it may mean the freeing of the ego in an ecstasy like the release of the soul in death.

"So it was that night. For Cléopâtre too. She was not a child nor had I known a woman until then. Such love is good, good for the psychic part of us. Half the neurasthenic ills of our generation are caused by its lack. The physical act alone is not enough, is nothing.

"We made love. We talked away the hours in between. If one can call such communion talk. The minutes raced through the night. The curtains were silhouettes against a shivering dawn.

"Then sitting up I said: 'Cléopâtre . . .' My words stumbled as they slipped from my throat. I did not want to speak then. I did not know I was going to speak then. If I had thought about it I could not have spoken, for it was wrong to smudge the beauty of the night by introducing considerations which had become both trivial and false. But the words came

[ 215 ]

forth, against my will. That happens sometimes. When we plan an action long in advance, and go over and over the details of our
procedure, the premeditated deed takes on a life
of its own; it acts through us. So sitting up I
said: 'Cléopâtre . . .' and looked at her face,
the eyes half closed, the lashes kissing her demure cheeks.

" 'Cléopâtre,' I said, 'I, whom you love, am
a Jew.'

"And with the words came a sharp internal
stab for now I, too, had killed.

"Her breathing became inaudible.

" 'Cléopâtre!' Her lashes lifted.

" 'John,' she said, 'why do you choose this
time to mock at me?' She smiled hopefully
and looked into my eyes.

"To my shame, I must confess that I was
tempted for an instant to accept her hint, and
pass off my remark as a joke.

"But my voice was answering for me.

" 'No, Cléopâtre,' it said, 'I am a Jew as my
father and my mother were before me.'

"She looked into my eyes, then turning her
face to the wall, began to shake. Her body was

convulsed as if a fit of violent laughter had seized upon her. I was frightened. Her restraint broke down.

"She *was* laughing.

"Peals of uproarious mirth shook the very walls. It was horrible. Nothing is more horrible than hysterical laughter."

Mercado waited for the paroxysm to subside. He lay beside her trying to unclench his hands. Fear chilled him; had she lost her mind? Now and then the spasms seemed to lessen. The laughter would change to a gurgle in a lower key, something like the weeping of a child who has lost control. Then, just as he was beginning to hope she was recovering, a fiendish countenance would turn full upon him. The inhuman expression would not alter, the eyes apparently did not see, but once more the hideous laughter, coming from within, would convulse its features.

Feeling that something was about to break inside himself, Mercado seized, in one heaving effort, her waving arms and tried to choke the spasms by the force of his embrace. It was as

[ 217 ]

if he grasped a struggling animal. He had lost all sense of her womanhood.

She was instantaneously still, though her muscles remained taut beneath his hands.

"Cléopâtre . . . dearest . . . I am no different.

"Cléopâtre!"

"Let me go . . . *cochon* . . . you lied. You have stolen . . . We Russians, we fight fair. We do not sneak from behind. We do not pretend love and stab . . . stab. We torture the bodies of our enemies, we do not destroy their souls. *Ah, salaud je m'en fous de toutes tes caresses.* Let go . . ."

Her shoulder and arm swung round with irresistible force. He was flung to one side. She fumbled with her bag on the night table.

"Take it . . ."

The knife gleamed in the pale light like a small trout as it leaps from a pool. Slowly it came toward him, the blade between her fingers, the hilt free for him to grasp.

"Take it . . . you have taken all but my life. My honor. My self-respect. Take my life too. I do not want it. It is no use to me now. What . . . are you afraid . . . dog!

You do not wish to imperil your skin. You throw dirt on my soul but take no chances with your little finger . . ."

Then, tearing her gown from the throat down, so that her breasts were bared:

"You will like the feeling. It goes in nicely. The warm blood, it gives life. I command you. It is my first request. You cannot refuse the one favor I ask. Press steadily. I promise you will like it. It is like making love, only more wonderful . . ."

Theatrical! The tearing of her dress made everything unreal.

Mercado took the knife, strode to the window, stepped on the balcony, and cast it into the moonlight. Like a flaming match dropped over a river, it fell into the black circle that had been a crimson flower bed, and was extinguished. Something went with it from himself.

"You . . you . . ."

She was sobbing. Now and then she uttered a short sentence in Russian. The words sounded piteous. He could not understand them. The same sounds repeated again and again. He had the impression she was appealing to her God.

He lit a cigarette. His hands were shaking. Daylight was slowly creeping into the corners of the room. An eternity seemed to pass. He finished his last cigarette. Still she lay there, talking to herself, softly sobbing.

He moved stealthily toward her. This could not last forever. He would go off his head. Violence was more easily borne. One did not have to think.

She was murmuring, but in a lower voice. He had to get close to hear. The words were French now.

"He's dead. If he were not dead he would come to me now. He's dead. If he were not dead he would come to me now. He's dead. If he were not . . ."

The monotone, without stress or break, was like the beat of a heart. He stretched out beside her.

A weak trembling hand started feeling its way toward him. He watched it as one watches a small blind kitten fumbling for its mother's teat. It touched his wrist and rested for a moment, apparently content. It crept up his arm, across his shoulder, along his neck. It paused for a moment on his eyesocket, then passed over his lips, as if with pleasure.

Suddenly a body was pressing close to him, winding its arms around him, sobbing, murmuring: "John, tell me where I am? Is it true something awful has happened? Have I lost my youth? John, I am afraid. Hold me, John."

He was far away. The pitiful, tear-streaked creature that was clinging to him bore no relation to the Cléopâtre whose embrace had set his blood on fire. He was sorry, with his intellect, for this incoherent creature. But that was all. He no longer felt. He could only listen, detached, weary . . .

"Speak to me, John. . . . Where have I been? I am an old woman. What has happened? John . . . beloved . . . speak to me."

He tried to comfort her as he would a child in pain. He smoothed her hair and whispered tender words. He hoped to conceal the emptiness of his gestures.

His attitude did not seem to matter. Apparently she was only conscious of his presence, not of his words or actions. Her lips were moving. He could hear the words again:

"I have loved. Love is terrible. It hurts me. You must never love, John. Be good to me but never love, never . . . never . . . never."

She was silent for a little while. Then she reached feebly, as if the effort were exhausting, for her pocket mirror. She looked steadily at herself in the glass for several seconds.

"It is true then. I am ten years older. My face is that of an old hag. Where has my youth gone, John? Have you taken it? What has happened to me? I have lost my youth. I am an old woman. John, speak to me. . . ."

He tried but she did not hear.

He spoke louder. False words of endearment which, once in the night, had been full of love, but now were empty. Perhaps she felt this, for she would not listen.

In desperation he took her head in his hands and attempted to kiss her lips. The fiendish light flashed into her eyes. She shook herself free. "What do you want?" she cried. "Who are you? Leave me alone. I am so afraid.

John, come to me, John, some one who pretends he is you won't leave me alone.  John . . ."

Then more quietly: "John is dead.  If he were not dead, he would come to me now. John is dead."

## CHAPTER ELEVEN

THEY had breakfast, strolled along the shore, sat for hours in the shade, and went rowing after luncheon, without discussing their situation or themselves. Now and then Mercado would catch her looking at him with puzzled eyes. She asked no questions. She assented, as if everything were of equal unimportance, to whatever he suggested. He looked up the hour at which they would have to leave in order to get to town for the night. She expressed no interest, and apparently did not notice that their week-end was being cut short.

However, when Mercado took her hand or made a perfunctory gesture of affection, she would draw away as if frightened. Her recoil was not brusque, in fact it was rather delicate, as if she did not want to hurt his feelings, but it gave him the impression that she felt he was a stranger and did not understand how she happened to be with him.

He was beyond suffering. One must still feel to suffer. Yet he would have given ten years of his life to be able to feel. The deadness, the desolation, the emptiness of walking like a ghost through a world of light and color, of tears and laughter, without reacting, was far worse than the terror and agony he had recently known.

Something was dead. His body was its grave. The flowers over the grave could not be smelt by the corpse within; nor could it hear the laments of the mourners.

He could not even feel remorse. He wondered at this; her words were seared into his brain, but he could evoke them without a shudder.

He returned to his room in the city after leaving Cléopâtre, and mechanically dropped into bed. His sleep was immediate and profound. His mind had been exhausted. Toward morning he became conscious of some one in the room, but he was not interested. However, the restless intruder was evidently bent on disturbing him, though for a long while he ignored its movements.

Finally it sat on his bed. He looked through

his lashes, pretending to be still asleep, at Vera. She noticed his slight movement: *"Où est Bill?"* Her deep voice sounded familiar. "What has become of him? He left me hours ago. John, tell me, where is Bill?"

She was insistent. He told her he did not know. She paced up and down, went out the door and returned, repeated her questions. He could not convince her of his sincerity. She evidently did not believe him.

Finally, after she had waked him several times, he lost his apathy and asked her what was the matter.

Bill had left her at the Caveau. She did not know why. Nothing had happened. She must see him before he sailed. She had something to say to him.

"Well," Mercado answered, "he's got to come back here. My trunk is packed but his isn't." And he turned over and would pay no further attention.

Not long afterwards he heard Halsey fumbling at the door. Vera gave a joyful cry and ran toward him. Mercado cursed them both, but slipped into his clothes while they were talking at the door and went downstairs for a cup of coffee. Bill's eyes were strange and his walk unsteady. Mercado, completely indifferent, only wanted to be left alone.

"How did you get here?" Halsey asked.

Vera was not rebuffed. She explained that the boy downstairs had given her the number of the room and that the door had been unlocked.

"Must pack," Bill said. "Why did John leave us?"

"Bill," she said, "I want to go with you. I can pay for my passage."

"They wouldn't let you in. It's hard for any Russian; impossible for an unattached lady."

"Make believe I'm your wife."

"No use. They read the passports."

"Bill, you've got to let me go with you. I won't bother you if you tire of me."

"Fine chance. . . . No. Impossible. Have to marry you. Impossible!"

Vera said nothing but looked at him.

"Small town. You don't know. Everybody gossips. Nothing done everybody doesn't know about. . . . No excitement, fun, drink.

Football games, lectures. . . . Students all over place.

"Can't be done. Would bore you to death. Cook your own meals. Mrs. Smith's word law. Propriety. Gloves and influenza. Isn't it just too lovely! Impossible! Can't even miss a bath without comment. 'No college spirit, he doesn't even watch football practice!' 'Did you notice Mrs. Seymour's new dress? She does look a freak. I was ashamed to be seen on the street with her.' Vera, I shall dream of you."

"Very well, Bill, but kiss me once more before you go."

He took her gingerly in his arms. Why couldn't she let him alone? It was hard enough without this . . .

When he was younger he had often dreamed of hanging from a precipice. A gulf had opened beneath him. If he let go . . . but he never did.

This time, with Vera in his arms, the vision was repeated. There was the rush of wind in his ears, the murmur of water far below. He must hold on. It would be pleasant to fall. To give up the struggle. To let himself go.

His fingers were clenched and aching. Why should he continue to fight? Was it worth the trouble?

He must hold on.

No. He couldn't.

"Good God, man, why aren't you packed?" Mercado's dull expression belied the emphasis of his question.

"I'm not going."

"Not going?"

"Not going." Halsey's voice was resigned and firm.

"All right," Mercado said, "you're not going."

He pulled out his suitcase and began packing the last odd articles. His lack of curiosity made Halsey feel as if he had just cracked a hollow nut. He didn't know what to make of it. He was prepared for a difficult argument in which his friend would have every advantage. Instead, Mercado did not even ask the reason for his altered plans.

"I'll miss the opening," Halsey remarked, after watching Mercado till he could no longer contain himself. "You'll make my excuses?"

"Of course," said Mercado. "Eloquently."

"Not too eloquently, please. I don't want to be suspended. Still, I'm not sure that I want to go back, not after this . . ."

"How soon can we expect you in Greensborough?"

"We'll sail in about ten days. That is, if . . . John, I'm going to be married."

"Congratulations."

Mercado was trying to close the clasp of his valise, which accounted, Halsey supposed, for this curious indifference. He waited a moment and then went on:

"Remember, John, how the girls would talk about going to Mexico and meeting bandits? We always laughed at them. Maybe they're right. Mexico, Peru, Australia, anywhere, anything, except Greensborough and going to tea with Mrs. Horace P. Smith. . . . Well, anyhow, I wouldn't have to lecture. I haven't made up my mind."

The valise snapped shut, Mercado rose.

"You'll come back," he said, "but you'll never get away in ten days. They say you can get a baby in France more quickly than you can get married, and with much less difficulty."

Not the suggestion of a smile on his face. No anger. Indifference. Suddenly he paused as if he had forgotten something, and turning toward Halsey, began to speak as if from memory:

"You evidently have swallowed the bait and been well hooked." On no other basis could he understand a cultured man's refusing to regard the possible outcome of his actions. He asked that his impertinence in requesting information should be excused. . . . He was repeating, gallingly, their old conversation. He finished: "I look forward to the dénouement with interest. Your taste, if I may use an expression of . . ."

He stopped as if something painful had occurred to him, then forced himself to go on: "Do I speak the truth?"

"I have regarded the outcome," Halsey objected. "I've probably thought about it a great deal more than you realize. Remember the arguments I adduced to prove that nothing would be more welcome in Greensborough than a Russian? Of course Vera will be welcome in Greensborough . . . that is, if we go back . . ."

Mercado interrupted. "It's all right, old man, I'm probably just jealous. Forget your defenses. Let's get out of here. The train doesn't go for three hours. We'll drink to the future."

"All right . . . but Vera's coming back."

"Where's she gone?" Mercado asked.

"I don't know."

"Leave word downstairs. Don't start by be-ing . . ."

A sharp rap at the door interrupted him—
*"Entrez! Entrez!"*

"Monsieur," announced the garçon from the depths of his dirty white jacket, "there is a gentleman below who insists on mounting. He sends his card."

Halsey examined it. A piece of limp paste-board about as large as a playing card which bore the superscription:

FYDOR STEFANOVICH DEMIDOFF
Commandant de Cosaques de
S.M.I. Nicolas II.

"The devil! That must be her brother. If only," Mercado added after a hasty survey of the disorderly interior, "he had come a few hours later. I won't see him."

"The Monsieur mounts after me," said the garçon.

"You talk to him, Bill. I've got to shave." Mercado spoke quickly. "Put him off. There's nothing more to be said." He grabbed the smallest of his valises and leaped into the bathroom just as Major Demidoff stepped through the door.

The Commandant glided by the *valet de chambre*, made a sweeping gesture with his small felt hat, placed it against his heart, and bowed low.

"It is indeed a pleasure," he murmured in a voice which was honeyed as a threat.

He was dark and very frail, the shadow of Cléopâtre. And rather shabby. "My sister," he explained, "has spoken of you—often. She has the highest respect, even affection. We Russians are sincere, ah, that is what you other Westerners will never understand."

"My friend and I are only professors of literature," Halsey replied. Evidently the Major had mistaken him for Mercado, but he had no desire to set the fellow right. He was very tired.

"A little drink, perhaps?" And he motioned to the bottle.

"Ah, no, my dear professor. Later, perhaps, but first there are things to explain. Will you take a seat? That is right. I prefer to stand. The room is small, but I can think of our free steppes.

"Can you picture for yourself our life in the open? From my earliest childhood I was taught to ride, to shoot. And with knives, ah, you cannot appreciate the skill we acquire. Thus"—drawing a blade from a sheath hidden beneath his armpit—"you observe the rosette of paper flowers on the wall. There! What strange taste the French have in decoration. Follow my hand. . . ."

The movement was very swift. He took the tip of the blade between his fingers, snapped his wrist, and . . . the tip of it dislodged a piece of plaster, some two inches below the paper rosette. The knife vibrated an instant in the wall, then fell to the floor with a clatter.

"A miss! My instructor, dear Anton Ivano-vich, would be very angry at such a fault.

[ 234 ]

However, it serves to demonstrate. And with the saber, almost an equal skill. But we were talking of my sister. What happens to me is of no importance. Life is over. But she has a child, but she must live. She has told you, perhaps, that I killed her husband. He was a brute.

"It is so difficult. She must dance and drink with strangers. To gain more than a bare living she would be forced to sleep with them. But that, ah, never. You appreciate her problems. For you, ah, my dear Professor, she has a real affection.

"A few . . ." He came to a stop before Halsey, "of your American banknotes, which go so far in Paris. No, not a check. We other Russians, checks we cannot understand. And even banknotes, in the old days it was only gold. But since the war . . .

"For me, life is over. I care not how it ends. In jail, in a quarrel, under the guillotine. But this has the air of a threat, and threats are not necessary with you, my dear Professor Mercado, for Clara has told me how you are *sympathique*. A few banknotes . . ."

Halsey rose and poured himself a drink with

a hand that barely trembled. He felt that everything was turning into farce and melodrama. These Russians had the gift of making melodrama convincing. Their life was keyed just one tone below hysteria. Was he right to marry Vera? Then he gulped down his doubts and the whisky together. "Demidoff," he said, "you're a bloody ass. My name isn't Mercado. Mercado has gone to the United States."

"But you are his friend, but you will help Clara, like him"—a little hysterically—"like him." The Commandant was reaching under his coat.

"Demidoff, don't be a fool. I haven't a cent. Besides, I'm marrying Cléopâtre's friend, the Countess Adranova, you know her?"

"What! *La Comtesse!* You are marrying *la Comtesse!*"

"I am about to marry the Countess," Halsey stiffened. He felt that the astonishment of the Major was, in some vague way, insulting. "I shall follow Mercado to the United States with my wife."

"But my dear fellow, accept my felicitations. You are stupendous, you Americans, such valor, you run off with our renowned *Comtesse*. How

THE PROFESSORS LIKE VODKA

she will be missed!  But, Monsieur . . ." and
the brave Commandant slumped into a chair.
His hat went sprawling across the floor, his
hands were raised to his eyes, his shoulders
heaved. . . . "What will my poor sister do?
This Mercado, he is a fool.  And you, you must
not speak of it."  For several minutes he remained silent, his eyes closed, his mouth con-
torted.

Halsey drained his glass, looked at his watch.
Vera was due any minute.  He wondered how
Mercado was getting on with his shave.  No
doubt he was cutting himself.  And how was he
going to get rid of the Major?  Perhaps, if he
pretended to leave . . .

"You will excuse me . . ."

"Wait!"  The officer straightened up, resum-
ing his dignity.  "You must not speak of this to
*Madame la Comtesse.*  My sister would never
forgive me.  Already I have hurt her.  She is
the soul of generosity.  She is too good for this
world.

"If she ever heard of this her heart would
break.  It is true she has to earn a living.  Yes;
but this, never!  She has told me nothing, noth-

[ 237 ]

ing, you understand. I have been watching, making—what do you say—inferences.

"I am in trouble. You other Americans, you do not understand what it is to be in trouble. To have everything. To have nothing. She would die rather than take money. If she knew of this! My poor little sister. You must save her at least from that. She is a Demidoff."

"I will never speak of it," Halsey promised.

"You will . . ."

"If I could get hold of this Mercado I would make him realize how he is honored to be the friend of my sister. Ah, but it is too late. Now you can only ruin me. . . ."

"I won't say a word. And, if you will excuse me?"

"*La Comtesse.*" The Major would not stop talking, "She is a woman. She has no doubt the best intentions. But women, they do not realize how much harm a little word may do. They are troubled by secrets. What they know squirms always to escape. My sister is terrible when she is angry. She has suffered much. She fears nothing. You must guard all this from *la Comtesse*. . . ."

Halsey had seen Vera approach. The Major

did not check his words until he felt her presence behind him. She had entered so silently.

"Fydor Stefanovich, what are you doing here?" she asked.

"I am come, *Madame la Comtesse,* to offer my felicitations. Clara has told me. I let no time slip . . ."

"Clara has told you?"

"Yes, she was so happy she could not wait to tell me."

"And how does she know?"

"She did not say but, I suppose, this Mercado, he has spoken of it."

"And how does he know?" Vera was insistent.

"I told him," Halsey interrupted. "He returned to get his things."

"He did not wait," Vera continued, "to say good-by to me? But his things are here! But you are not clever, you, *mon cher* Beelly, you think you can conceal . . . but where is he?"

Halsey had gradually edged around the room until he was behind the Major. He tossed several imaginary medicine balls toward the door trying, by this gesture, to let Vera know that it was important to get rid of the officer. He was

[ 239 ]

unable to make out whether or not she understood, for she had dropped into Russian.

The Major answered her in the same tongue. She seemed rather excited, but that was not unusual and often meant nothing at all.

Meanwhile Mercado had been lathering his face. He heard, through the warped door, much of what was said. At first he had been tempted to come out. He had felt cowardly, evading his responsibilities by hiding himself. However, when he grasped the purport of the visit, he was so elated by his escape from what seemed to have been a deliberate plot that he forgot his equivocal position. He wanted to laugh. He made grimaces at the mirror. Some of the foam got into his mouth. Life was a roaring farce. Only fools were serious. Soap looked more appetizing than it tasted. "I, whom you love . . ." He would never believe any one again. He would laugh at them all.

A change in the tempo of the talk brought him back to the door. ". . . would never forgive me. Soul of generosity . . . if she ever heard of this her heart would break. . . ."

Damn it! Mercado looked at his eyes. His whitened face was a grotesque mask. Gorilla!

He stared into his eyes. "Her heart would break!" He had known it all along and yet had jumped, on the flimsiest of evidence, to the absurd conclusion that their romance had been a commonplace conspiracy. The brother was probably mad. No wonder Cléopâtre distrusted life. He must shave. Afterwards he would come out and face the scoundrel.

Deliberately, holding the razor at an acute angle against his skin, he scraped away at his beard. He was proud of his steadiness.

"He will tell me nothing, Beell, but I know no good brought him here." Thus Vera summed up her conversation with the Commandant.

The latter had fallen back into his chair and was now solemnly tapping a cigarette on the palm of his left hand. He was evidently aware that his presence was irritating to Halsey and intended to extract all the amusement he could from this fact.

"This Mercado," he drawled, "belongs, I suppose, to one of your good families."

"In America," Halsey answered, "there are no distinctions between families."

"Yes," said the Major, "I have heard it is a country without an aristocracy. That, I find, very curious. One goes to a party and sits beside the grocer's wife. It is thus from necessity that conversation has been eliminated and Americans tell instead what they call funny stories. Is it not so? I have listened to these funny stories often. They are *drôle*, is it not so? I have often wondered . . ."

Again a knock on the door. "It's me, Fanny Cumberland. Can I came in, come in, come in?"

"Come on in," shouted Halsey, who had begun to appreciate that the situation had a humorous side and rather welcomed this new diversion. Fanny, the Quarter's ambulant joke, was accepted because her effervescing kindliness precluded a brutal rebuff while her obtuseness made her unconscious of gentler measures. She bubbled continuously. Her tautological hat, bosom and verbiage were difficult to ignore. She advanced, with her hot potato roll, speaking. . . .

"You're leaving, leaving, leaving, Julien told

me.  You should throw a party, make a night
of it.  Every one's been asking what's happened
to you and I didn't know, didn't know, couldn't
tell them. . . ."

She paused, realizing she was before two
strangers who were standing up to be presented.
Then went on:

"Delighted to meet you; where is John; I
thought you were leaving—*enchanté, Monsieur,
enchanté, Madame; I didn't know* . . ."  Her
eyes expressed wonder at meeting foreigners in
an American's room.  She caught enough of
their names to grasp their nationality.

"Russian!  How lovely!  Russians always
like me!  A Cossack told me with the most gorgeous eyes that I had a Russian soul.  I didn't
know what he meant!"  She smiled widely.
"He felt, of course, the sympathy, the compre-
hension . . . but where is John?  I have news,
you must help me, help me; it's Sam Hewitt;
you know Sam, don't you, Bill?  Sam's in trouble, in trouble.  I thought going back you might
do something.  But I want John to hear, too.
Where is John?"

"Won't you sit down?" suggested Vera.

"A lovely Russian girl downstairs, lovely

Russian girl," Fanny continued; "no, thank you, followed me in." The Major snapped out of his amused air of toleration. "I heard her asking if a Russian officer had gone upstairs, upstairs. I did not think, but meeting you all here made me think, made me wonder. . . . But where is John, where is John? I want him to hear about Sam. . . ."

"What did she look like?" asked Bill.

"He has been ordered to leave, to get out inside of three weeks; it's so unfair, so terrible; he did nothing, nothing really, and he has no money, no place to go."

She hesitated, obviously overcome by her feelings. The Major seized the opportunity to recover his hat.

"You will kindly excuse me," he said, "for paying so short a visit. I have an appointment, most important which . . ." The door, toward which he was rapidly backing, opened:

"*Bonjour*, Bill, I did not want you to leave without my good wishes for a pleasant journey."

"Cléopâtre!" he stuttered.

She was shaking hands with Vera and her brother as if she had expected to find them there. Fanny was surveying the new arrival with her mouth silently open.

"It is very good, this news I hear," Cléopâtre was addressing Bill again. "I am so happy for you. You will have a wonderful life together in America, and Vera . . ." Halsey was annoyed; he could not understand the rest of what she said.

Meanwhile Mercado was steadying himself. His heart had bounded so violently when he heard Cléopâtre's voice that he had hardly been able to breathe. He had to wait a moment before advancing. If only the damned Commandant, he thought, had not put in an appearance. He wanted to look into her eyes again.

He regarded himself in the glass. His face was clean, his hair neat. It must be gone through. He had asked big moments of life. Would she speak to him? Their parting had been a farewell. He had thought all was over. Her concierge must have told her that her brother had asked for his address, and she had followed after to prevent trouble. Well . . . no, he could not say what he wanted. If the brother had not tried to force his hand he might have reconsidered. But now . . . nothing left but to keep his self-respect and carry on. Hateful word that, but one cannot always choose.

He was standing at the door in full view.

No one seemed to be looking at him.

"John." It was Fanny of course who broke the tension. "Sam Hewitt's been expelled, run out of France for carrying a penknife, for carrying a penknife. . . ."

"I suppose," the Major stood stiffly, "I have the honor of addressing Professor Mercado."

"You've only got an hour to make the train." Halsey's voice was dry, business-like. He had edged over toward Vera and had taken her arm.

"I am delighted." Mercado's bearing was anything but cordial. "Cléopâtre has spoken of you often."

The Major surveyed him leisurely through his glass, then asked: "May I have the favor of a few words?"

Mercado automatically assented while his eyes rested on Cléopâtre.

"I think," she was saying, "that there will hardly be time enough for Professor Mercado to make his boat as it is. Come, Fydor, I want you to take me home."

"Monsieur," the Commandant went on unperturbed, "would you do me the honor of listening to a few words? If you prefer to hear them in public I shall not be averse." His voice was pitched in a high querulous key.

"Fydor!" Both Vera and Cléopâtre addressed him at the same time. Both stopped short in order to permit the other to continue. The Major's words ran on suavely:

"Monsieur, as you are an American, one does not expect from you chivalry or honor, nevertheless . . ."

Mercado's face was white. He stared rigidly at the Major, who suddenly began to gesticulate, and to contort his meager angular form as if possessed. Cléopâtre was trying to grasp her brother's arm and was muttering in Russian.

"As you are in my room," Mercado carried it off well, "temporarily my guest, I can only ask you to get out." He seemed cool and collected. He was thanking the fate that permitted him to talk English. The Major was evidently fluent in that tongue, for he continued, more calmly:

"There are certain decencies not even an

American can violate with impunity. Fortunately I am come to demand an accounting. Though we Russians have lost our country, we treasure our pride. Monsieur, after what has occurred, do you still propose to leave for America without . . ."

"My plans," Mercado's manner was ponderous, "concern no one but myself and Cléopâtre." He turned toward the latter. His eyes came to life. They seemed to be searching for something lost. But his voice was dead.

"You consider, I suppose, our parting to have been final?" He had put the question so that only one answer was possible. He realized this as he heard his words. His eyes were doomed to search in vain. Grief flowed out from his heart, blurring his vision. It was the end.

Then he remembered the Major. Perhaps he would have to fight a duel. But the choice of weapons would be his. Baseball bats at two paces. Or they could enter a wood from different sides and stalk for each other. That would be a sensation! He'd have at least half a chance. No fencing for him.

As for her . . . she flickered like a match's flame . . . that was the trouble . . . he could never see her steady . . . always, even as he looked, she became something else. . . .

"I suppose," he repeated his words, "you consider our parting to have been final."

"*Absolument!*"

She had trouble getting out the word, though it did not lack for emphasis. Then, in a tired voice, turning to her brother, she said: "Fydor, I am bored, take me home."

At this the Major began to laugh. He twisted himself half round and addressed the bystanders.

"My sister," he said, "is so hard to please. Last time she was, what you say, flying the coop. This time it is Monsieur who is going away. It is *rigolo*, is it not so? But my duty now is clear for every one to see.

"Monsieur." He drew himself up and confronted Mercado once more. "Monsieur, you will have to postpone for a little your sailing. If you will. . . ." He was taking a large brown wallet from his inside pocket. A silver coat of arms adorned the upper corner. Fanny, who had been suffering all this while from her inability to participate, suddenly dashed forward with a "How lovely! Such a cute little unicorn!  Do let me look at it, Mr. Demiruff; I just love unicorns. . . ."

A nervous laugh ran round the circle.

The Commandant, checked for the instant, was grasped again by Cléopâtre, who whispered something in his ear.  For the second time he perceptibly collapsed, although he managed to remain on his feet.

"In that case," he continued, "I cannot meet you on the field of honor.  However, I shall take pleasure . . ."

Cléopâtre had at last succeeded in silencing him.  His strength had left him.

"Monsieur," she turned to Mercado, "you are most unfortunate.  I am sorry for you."

She started with her brother for the door.

Mercado forgot, as she spoke, his quandary. He had been debating whether he should knock the Major down or let him go in peace.

Her words arrested him.  What did she mean?  He wanted to speak to her alone.  This was no way to part.

"Cléopâtre!"  He uttered her name.  It quivered in the hushed room.  He realized too late he had made a mistake.

"Monsieur."  She stared through him as if

she were freezing an importunate beggar. His softness had broken against her tight-pressed lips. She was replying, but not to him. To the room! To the world!

"Le Monsieur, I am sorry for him. He was cursed before he came into the world. What he can have he does not want. It is most unfortunate. He is accursed. It is but a kindness when we remove him and his kind from the earth.

"Fydor, let us go."

The brother and sister were walking quietly toward the door, chatting in their own language, apparently unconscious that any one they knew was within a hundred miles.

"Madame," Mercado said, making a theatrical bow to the two moving figures, "I shall ever be in your debt for a most enchanting week-end."

Why had he said that? He was disgusted with himself. The brother and sister passed out of the room. The door closed.

"John," Fanny gasped hysterically, "the penknife was a frame-up, frame-up. Sam got stewed and got in bed with the wife of the concierge. And she wouldn't appear against him, against him. So they framed him with my penknife. My little penknife, I gave it to him. They called it a weapon. John you will do something, do something. He has no money, nothing. Write to the papers, write your congressman, do anything you can."

"With pleasure," Mercado answered, "I'll do anything I can."

**THE END**

# *Afterword*

## BY HAROLD LOEB

THE beginnings of my second novel, *The Professors Like Vodka,* are obscure. I do not know precisely when I wrote it, where I wrote it, or why I wrote it. However, these unknowns can be delimited by recalling the events of the years between my first novel, published in 1925, and my third, published in 1929.

*Broom,* the European magazine of international art and letters which I founded and edited, folded in Berlin when my money gave out with the March number in the spring of 1923. Kitty Cannell, who had helped especially with the translations, and I returned to Paris where she found a flat in Montmartre on the Rue Blanche. I remember the draperies were heavy and I did not like the sounds of night life outside the windows. Matthew Josephson, my last associate editor, had already gone back to America. Malcolm Cowley, who had contributed poetry, several fictive prose portraits, and much good advice, completed his studies in the south of France and rented rooms above a blacksmith shop in Giverney, near the Seine, which Claude Monet and other Impressionists had popularized.

## THE PROFESSORS LIKE VODKA

I remember a visit to Giverney when Dos Passos, E. E. Cummings, and Louis Aragon were Cowley's other guests. On that rainy night, they burned a quantity of books, paperbacks, mostly French, and the *Revue Française*. The lot were piled in the middle of the room and set on fire. I did not assist wholeheartedly because I felt that bad books should be published as well as good books for those who liked to read bad books. Then they put out the fire by urinating on it. Perhaps we had drunk too much. Afterward, Malcolm and I wrestled in the rain on the wet earth. The battle went on interminably. He was strong as a bear. I could not throw him because he was too strong. He could not throw me because I knew how to wrestle, having been on the team at Princeton, and was too agile.

A week later, Kitty asked me what I was going to do now that *Broom* was finished.

I said, "Write a novel."

She said, "You can't just sit down and write a novel."

"Why not?" I asked.

"Not everyone can write," she said.

"Anyone can write one novel," I hesitated, "though not everyone can write a good novel."

So, I started the story which came to be known as *Doodab*. Meanwhile, Matty had begun to republish *Broom* in New York, largely with the material left over from Berlin. In August 1923 I mailed him the first chapter of *Doodab* which he accepted and sent to the printer. I forwarded the second chapter. He hesitated over it and I asked him to send it all back. Eventually, Harold Stearns asked if he could submit the manuscript to Horace Liveright. I agreed and was delighted when the young publisher accepted my first novel by telegram if I would replace the "a's" and "the's" which I had eliminated whenever I thought they were functionless.

This must have been the fall of 1923 or winter of 1924 because I remember doing the second chapter of my novel *Doodab* in a village near Giverney where I was all alone, the Cowleys having left on July 14 for America. After a few days trying to converse with the local inhabitants in my primitive French, I gave up and walked over to Giverney. Cowley's apartment was now occupied by Robert Coates, who had written several stories for *Broom,* and Elsa, his wife. They put me up and I played tennis on the public courts, gradually regaining my former skill.

Meanwhile, Kitty had run into Ford Madox Ford on the terrace of the Dôme. She had known him in London. He was living with Stella Bowen, a hearty, loud-voiced Australian who no longer appreciated Ford's rambling, inaccurate, but wonderful literary anecdotes. Ford invited us to his next tea party at the office of the *transatlantic review* on an island in the Seine. It was there that I met Ernest Hemingway, who had begun to assist on the *transatlantic.* Afterward, Ernest and I played tennis on many an afternoon, and boxed afterwards. Gradually, he and his friends filled the gap left by the departure of Cowley and Josephson.

We decided to go skiing together in Austria that winter, and to Pamplona in July to see the bullfights about which he was enthusiastic. Gertrude Stein had first put the idea in his head and the year before a group had gone which included Bob McAlmon, Donald Ogden Stewart, a couple of whose ribs were broken, John Dos Passos, Bill and Sally Bird, George O'Neil, an English soldier named Dorman-Smith, Ernest and his wife Hadley.

In December 1924, Hemingway, Hadley, and Bertrim and Gusta Hartman went off on schedule to go skiing at Schruns. I stayed behind, torn between the desire to go with them and anxiety over the manuscript of *Doodab.* After some hesitation, I left at Christmastime for New York instead of for Austria, and put up at the Princeton Club and then at my brother's who was living on West 74th Street. I could not have begun *The Professors Like Vodka* at this time because the episode on which it was based did not occur until the following summer. Apparently, I occupied myself putting the "a's" and "the's" back into *Doodab* and floating around New York during this middle prohibition period.

New York was gay but different from Paris, largely because the people I knew spent more money. Liquor was expensive and everything that went with it. To know the right speakeasies became important. And we danced a lot. I met among others Beatrice and George Kaufman, Peggy Leach, the Herbert Swopes, Paul Robeson, and the Marx brothers. By and large I enjoyed myself, until I joined a poker game and lost some $20-30. This seemed too much and I confined myself thereafter to more social amenities.

*Doodab* went to press that spring. I was fortunate also to

catch Hemingway's manuscript of *In Our Time* as it was being mailed back to him by Beatrice Kaufman, who was reading for Liveright. Sherwood Anderson also put a good word in for it. Since Sherwood was Liveright's leading literary author at the time, the stories were accepted and I wired Hem. He also received the news from Don Stewart and wrote back a letter of thanks. The correspondence is in the Princeton University Library.

I returned to Paris in the spring after several urgent pleas from Kitty. She had found two adjoining flats on the Rue Montessuy. Bill Smith, Hem's longtime friend from Michigan whose sister Kate had introduced Hadley to Hem, had already arrived. This improved the tennis, since Bill and I were a good match for Hem and Paul Fisher who was by far the best player on the court. Nevertheless, I accepted an invitation from my cousin Peggy Guggenheim, and went to the house she had rented near Deauville where she and her husband, Laurence Vail, were spending the summer. Kitty joined us there and was trapped in some quicksand, but got out all right.

Later I joined my mother in London for a short visit. She was staying at the Berkeley and put me up in a small room on Half Moon Street where every morning a charming young woman brought me tepid scrambled eggs and terrible British coffee. Aunt Florette who was living across the way at Claridge's and had married a Guggenheim, one of my mother's brothers, used to commiserate with my mother whom she said could not put up at Claridge's because I was failing to support her in the style to which she was accustomed. It may have been on this visit that I met Stephen Hayden Guest, son of a Member of Parliament, and his mother and stepfather, Dr. and Mrs. Eder, enthusiastic Zionists. Also I began to think about a second novel. *Doodab,* though reviewed well enough, was not having much of a sale.

On returning to Paris, I became aware of Duff Twysden whom I had been seeing here and there in the Quarter before I left for New York. Her musical laugh, even though it was not loud, could be heard above the café's uproar. One evening, we spoke to each other as described in my memoir *The Way It Was.* A few days later, Duff and I left for St. Jean de Luz.

Duff returned to Paris in some two weeks and then I received a letter from her asking if I minded her coming to Pamplona with my friends Hemingway and Bill Smith. And with Pat Guthrie, whom she intended to marry.

I wrote back that I could take it if she could.

We all met at Pamplona for the Fiesta. Eventually, the party broke up. Hem and Hadley went on to Madrid. Bill Smith, Duff, Pat, and I went back to Paris. I don't know where Don went. Kitty would have nothing more to do with me so it happened that Bill Smith and I, at the suggestion of Paul Fisher went one night to the Caveau Ukranien [actually the Caveau Caucasien] and bought drinks for a Comtesse Vera and a Princess Cléopâtre, as described in *The Professors Like Vodka.* It was great fun. Vodka by the carafe makes an excellent beverage.

I remember one morning when we found ourselves in a rowboat on a lake in the Bois de Boulogne. Everyone was high and the sun was up too. Cléopâtre liked to row. It became a routine. We quickly acquired the habit of arriving at the Caveau toward evening and staying up all night. It was quite the most prolonged binge I ever indulged in and, I admit, I enjoyed it. Other details are given in *The Professors Like Vodka.*

Oddly though, our bicycle trip in search of the Rhine was barely mentioned in the book. We, Bill and I, had decided for reasons of health and education to go looking for the Rhine on bicycles. A reserved, unpretentious fellow, given to long silences and occasional wisecracks, he was a good companion and we had become close friends—a friendship that was to last a long time, until his death in early 1972.

In the book, the long coast downhill from the Vosges Mountains was touched upon, but little else. We gave up our bicycles at a border town near Baden Baden. It was pouring rain and the German or French authorities, probably the German, wanted us to put up a deposit. Eventually, we did hand over some $20 and never got the money back, a fact Bill Smith remembered for many years. We took a train down the Rhine Valley and spent at least one night at Wörms, although I did not visit the Jewish cemetery where presumably my ancestors had been buried for some thousand years. Carlos Baker stated in his biography of Hemingway that we did not reach Wörms, which had been our goal. He was wrong.

Afterward we went back to Paris, the Caveau Ukranien, the Comtesse and the Princesse. The Comtesse Vera became infatuated with Bill, but he seemed immune to women. I was more than ever fascinated by the Princesse Cléopâtre, particularly by her large, powerful hands which could crush mine, even though I had been a wrestler at college.

Cléopâtre had enjoyed riding with her father's troop during the revolution and killing Jews, who were to her not quite people, by embracing them with a dagger between her breasts. Since I was a Jew, I found this attitude, shall I say, ironic? I knew that someday I would tell her I was a Jew. It was only a question of when. Finally I did.

Nothing further happened except the episode described in the novel, and the renewed consciousness of being a Jew which previously had been somewhat intermittent. Though I had been aware of it since childhood when there seemed to be some question as to whether or not we could get a hotel room on the right or left bank of the river that flows into Lake Lucerne, in general I did not think the matter concerned me. I was conscious of being a Jew at school and again at college as all or nearly all Jews are, but I did not waste thought on a situation about which I could do nothing. I thought of Jewishness as being a distinction as well as a handicap. The Eders, Stephen Guest and now Cléopâtre helped to change this.

There was no sequel to the episode, except for one evening several years later, when I was showing my sister-in-law the sights of Paris. Harry Frank, my sister-in-law's brother, had been a drummer in the Princeton band and liked to take over this instrument whenever the opportunity permitted. Consequently, we were sitting close to the orchestra at the Caveau Ukranien when suddenly the Comtesse Vera came up from behind and with a resounding right swing knocked me off my stool. Harry thought this was very funny and beat the drum thereafter with added gusto.

Although I never saw Cléopâtre again and had little desire to see her again, her character fascinated me. As mentioned above, the strong grip of her hand impressed me no end, and her open love of killing, deplorable as I felt it to be, was obviously sincere, so I invented the brother to help with the story's denouement and put the rest down from memory as best I could.

I may have started *The Professors Like Vodka* after the scene with Cléopâtre in the late summer of 1925. Afterward, Bill and I returned to New York on the S.S. *Suffren* and Bill went back to Provincetown where he joined up with his sister and her friends. It does not seem likely that I scribbled at night during our bicycle trip. I suppose I must have worked on it on my return to New York in my brother's house where I had a room of my own.

In the spring, I returned to Paris partly to see Duff with whom I had been corresponding. On the night of my arrival, she was at the Select with Lett Haines and had been drinking too much. I left at once and took a room at the Hotel Montparnasse. Then, having made the acquaintance of a character from Broadway, with wide shoulders and black side-whiskers, and Nicky, a pretty blonde from Vlissengen, Holland, I purchased a secondhand car and wandered with them for several weeks through the south of France. Finally, becoming tired of continuous travel, Nicky and I settled down in St. Paul de

Vence in a farmhouse surrounded by an artichoke field. Every morning I picked two artichokes, not realizing that their price would appear later added to the rent.

It may only have been at this time that I started working on *The Professors Like Vodka,* which described our taking out the two Russian women. Life on the Riviera was pleasant enough though somewhat monotonous. Blanche Hayes, Peter Grim, and others whom I had known in the past came to stay at the hotel on the hill, but for the most part I remained in the valley and worked.

In any case, I know that the manuscript was completed by midwinter 1926, because Malcolm Cowley had the kindness to come with me at this time to Asbury Park to go over it. It seemed odd revisiting this resort city with such a serious purpose in mind. I had known Asbury Park since childhood, as a place one went to ride on the ferris wheel or in one of the boats of the Old Mill. In the winter time, the quieter town had a different character. The book was published by Liveright in 1927.

It was while on the artichoke farm that I read *The Sun Also Rises.* It annoyed me, but I did not think of it as anti-semitic. Certainly, Hemingway was out to get Robert Cohn and Robert Cohn was Jewish, but Hemingway for the most part used Bill Gorton who was supposed to be based on Bill Smith or Donald Ogden Stewart or both of them to express anti-semitism. Both Bill Smith and Donald Ogden Stewart were to marry Jewish wives and live happily with them ever after. I learned to like them both and I never knew gentiles less touched with anti-semitism. They were nice men, too.

Barnes, the hero of *The Sun Also Rises,* who presumably was based on Hemingway, also is supposed by many commentators to hate Jews. However, I saw a great deal of Hem for over a year without ever having observed a touch of this prevalent prejudice, except for the episode with Leon Fleischman described in *The Way It Was.* And I understood only too well how Hem felt at that moment. Whatever the effects of *The Sun Also Rises,* which certainly shocked me, isolated as I was amongst the artichokes in the south of France, it did not have an influence on my writing nor later do I think it was a serious factor in my decision to visit Israel—or Palestine as it was then called.

Stephen Guest became a good friend for many years. Later he became fanatical about Marxism and the coming revolution, but his parents remained steadfast and earnest Zionists, prominent in the movement until they died. They introduced me to Herbert Weizman and other prominent Zionists. These contacts gave my experience with Cléopâtre a special poignancy.

On the other hand, I do not think the religious aspect of Judaism had any bearing on my renewed interest in Jews and Judaism. Rather it was the romantic ideal which evoked my interest. I read many books on the kibbutzim, and the history of the Jews from Josephus on. Also there was a vague memory, come down from a Miss Clemens engaged in my childhood to familiarize me with Judaism, of the heroic Maccabees and their war of freedom against the Greeks. These stories had inspired me at the time and no doubt their memory turned me now toward the Near East.

Consequently, I think it was the dedication of the Eders and the blood lust of Cléopâtre rather than the Jewish problem which induced me to write *The Professors Like Vodka* and later turned my thoughts toward Israel.

In any case, I took a ship to Tel Aviv by way of Alexandria in the autumn of 1927 leaving Nicky, the Dutch girl, with my mother who was in Paris at the Crillon Hotel with her new husband. My mother enjoyed Nicky who had a flair for attracting men to their table.

I arrived in Tel Aviv in the winter and went to Jerusalem where I put up in a boarding house occupied for the most part by American and English Jews. For awhile it was pleasant enough sightseeing in this land so reminiscent of biblical days, with the Arab women swathed from head to foot and the camels striding softly along the narrow alleys with bells tinkling on their toes. After a few months, however, I became lonesome for Nicky and asked her if she would bring the car to Beirut, which she gladly did. It was a pleasure once again to drive and I became interested in the desert. It was sparsely inhabited by the Druse who had been fighting the French army, but I understood that conditions were relatively peaceful by then and that as Americans we would have no trouble with either side.

After resting a few days in Beirut, I suggested that we return to Israel by way of Damascus and the desert where the Druse lived. When I broached this idea to Nicky, she clapped her hands and seemed overly delighted. So we spent a pleasant month in the hill country and the desert before crossing Jordan and returning to Palestine by way of Galilee. Some time in this period I began working on my third novel, *Tumbling Mustard.*

Probably it was during this time that I became enthusiastic about the transformation of the Jews in Palestine. Instead of the downtrodden-looking, sidewalk people to whom I was accustomed in New York and elsewhere, they seemed to have vitality which I had not encountered before and a desire to overturn mountains if it were necessary.

No doubt it was then that I really became imbued with Zionist ideals. But *The Professors Like Vodka* had already been written. So we will have to put the responsibility for my interest in the subject primarily on Cléopâtre.

In the autumn of 1928 I returned to New York and immediately went down to see my old friend Malcolm Cowley who had become the literary editor of the *New Republic,* and asked him if he would like an article on Zionism and the Near East. He was willing to let me write on the subject though somewhat skeptical of my competence, and it was in the fall of 1928 that I did two articles on Zionism both of which received a good response. Afterward, I wrote a series of articles for Jimmy Wise who was editing a Zionist periodical called, I think, *Opinion.*

Then I became interested in economics since it seemed

important in the early thirties and got from Jacob Baker and Harry Hopkins the means to do a research called *The National Survey of Potential Product Capacity.*

It was a long time before I returned to novel writing.

Harold Loeb

Weston, Connecticut.
August, 1973

*Textual Note:* The text of *The Professors Like Vodka* published here is a photo-offset reprint of the first printing (New York: Boni & Liveright, 1927). No emendations have been made in the text.

M. J. B.